ON WHETSDAY

MARK SUMNER

Word Posse

Acknowledgements

My thanks to Tom Drennan, Laurell K. Hamilton, Rett Macpherson, Deborah Millitello, and Sharon Shinn for their help in putting this into shape. Special thanks to Marella Sands, who not only helped with the manuscript but did yeoman work in turning that manuscript into this book. Additional thanks to Susan Gardener, Barbara Morrill, Laura Clawson, Vicki Grove, and Markos Moulitsas Zuniga at Daily Kos, who surrendered space on the front page and got the Saturday evening installments of the serial up on time even when I was late. It's all an experiment. Now let's go check the results.

Interior artwork for *On Whetsday* was created by Amy Jones. The cover for this edition is from Brian Zick. Both Amy and Brian stepped forward with fantastic work even when the whole project looked rather shaky. I love all of it, would recommend either of them for anything, and no, I will not say which of them was more accurate in drawing a cithian.

From Word Posse

Sleeping the Churchyard Sleep, Rett MacPherson
Pandora's Mirror, Marella Sands
Fortune's Daughter, Marella Sands
Restless Bones, Marella Sands
The Water Girl, Deborah Millitello
Do Virgins Taste Better? And Other Strange Tales, Deborah Millitello
Thor McGraw and the Ice Man Murder, Tom Drennan
The Naturalist, Mark Sumner
On Whetsday, Mark Sumner

Visit us at www.wordposse.com

ISBN-10: 0-9908392-9-X
ISBN-13: 978-0-9908392-9-3

I

WHETSDAY

On Whetsday, Denny danced at the spaceport. It was a good place to dance, if you didn't mind the heat that boiled off the acres of asphalt or the noise of the rising shuttles. You could meet a dozen races in single morning: lithe little skynx, scarlet klickiks, and sluggish chugs with their curtains of eyes brushing the ground. Most of the passing visitors had never seen a human, and fewer still understood what Denny was doing. Dancing was a rare thing among the races of the galaxy. But they understood enough to toss shiny credit chips or small bits of scrip into the box by his feet. They understood begging. Begging was universal.

Cousin Kettle had told everybody that Denny was not a very good dancer, but Denny didn't let that opinion slow his feet. Kettle had a job helping out at the port, a very responsible position for a human; though the truth was Kettle just cleaned food troughs, and scrubbed fouled pacer bays, and carried stuff. When Denny came to dance at the port, the door guards would sometimes come out to watch, but Kettle stayed away. Denny could tell that Kettle was embarrassed.

Most of the guards were lesser dasiks, and Denny thought that they liked his dancing. The speech badges clipped to the dasiks' uniforms were coded only with phrases like "do not cross the green line" and "present your identification," so he could not be sure, and the dasiks never dropped a chip in Denny's box, but when they passed him, they would often pause and watch. The dasiks were very tall, and everything about them was long. Long feet. Long hands. Long faces. When they watched Denny dance, their long necks swung from side to side and their long mouths opened to reveal double rows of long needlely teeth. They never once pressed the button that said "leave this area immediately."

Close to noon, when the dull red sun and the tiny blue-white sun were so tight together in the sky that everything at the port cast one set of deep violet-fringed shadows, a very old chug came out of the main terminal in a burst of cold ammonia-scented air. Denny could tell it was very old because, even though the eyes at the top of the chug were still rich shades of brown, and blue, and orange, those at the bottom had turned dead white. Some of the stalks were even missing their eyes altogether.

Denny could see some of the chug's many limbs swaying and clicking though the gaps left by the missing eyes.

One of the dasiks put its long head through the terminal door after the chug and pressed the button that said, "Follow the blue dots to the air taxi." The chug angled a dozen brown eyes at the pavement, and it shuffled forward as if it were going to comply with this advice. The guard clicked his long teeth together and went back inside. As soon as the door closed, a cluster of orange eyes tipped Denny's way, and the chug stopped.

Already there were a dozen chips gathered at the bottom of Denny's box, and the Whetsday heat was scorching. Normally, he would have been thinking about going home, but this was the first real audience of the day—the first person to truly stop for him instead of just tossing a chip—and he wanted to put on a good show. He raised the volume of his singing and the energy of his dance. He clapped his hands, which made the brown eyes jerk away, and stomped his feet, which made the blue eyes open wide, and sang "all alone, Old Poppa Stone, rolling home." He rose up onto his toes and spun around.

A ripple went through all the eyes. "You a human?" said the chug. Its voice was soft and windy and it was hard to tell what part of the chug produced the sound, but it spoke Xetosh very well.

Denny stopped singing and tipped down from his toes. "Yes," he said. "That's right."

There was a skittering, clicking sound from somewhere beneath the eyes, as if a number of tiny metal switches were being thrown very quickly. Four blue eyes raised up and looked toward the distant city, six brown eyes directed themselves at the door to the terminal. The cluster of orange eyes kept their gaze on Denny. "I understood that humans were not allowed out of the containment facility."

"The containment facility?" Denny had never heard anyone call part of Jukal Plex a "facility," but after a moment's thought he smiled. "Do you mean the human quarter?" He glanced back over his shoulder. The tallest buildings of the plex were clear on the skyline, with the great pale spike of the Cataclysm standing above all the rest, but the buildings near the human quarter were shorter, and Denny could not make them out.

The quarter itself was far too small to spot. Despite the name, it wasn't a fourth of the great city, or even a four hundredth. It was just a few buildings, a few streets and a handful of compartment houses, most of them empty. Like everything else about humans, once it had been more important. "When there were lots of humans, we used to have to stay in the quarter—you know, so we didn't get in the way," Denny explained. "Now that the cithians have consigned most of us on to other cities, they let us move around more."

"How many?" asked the chug.

"What?"

"How many humans?"

"In Jukal?" Denny had to think for a moment. "Fifteen. No...thirteen. Auntie Jo and her baby went off last month."

There was some rustling among the eyes, and more than a few of the stalks twined around each other as brown eyes turned to look into orange eyes and blue stared into blue. "So few?" There was more of that switchy clicking and clacking.

"That's just in Jukal," Denny said with a shrug. "People get moved. Anyhow, there used to be more."

"Yes," said the chug. "There did." It waved toward Denny's feet with a twitch of multicolored eyes. "What is this thing you do?"

"Dancing."

"Is it a human thing?"

"Yes. I've heard that the skynx dance too, but not like humans."

"Dance like a human," said the chug. A hundred eyes tilted toward Denny. "I want to see a human thing."

Denny grinned. He didn't think the chug was making fun of him. It was dangerous to read emotions into races you didn't know well, but he thought the old chug seemed sad. Perhaps if he danced well enough, the chug might toss a red chip, or even a blue.

He tilted back his head and sang, "Hey Judy, hey Judy, hey" to the hard white sky. He shook out his shoulders, and flung up his arms. He let a wave move through him that curved his neck, then his back, then his hips, then his knees, and then his feet. Left, right, left again. He sang the old music and tossed himself this way with a "hey" that way with a "Judy." He shook his head at the part about being "sad," and nodded when the song got to "better, better, better." The two suns were straight overhead, red touching blue, and the heat made sweat roll down Denny's face. In the near distance, a shuttle shot upward with a rumble that shook the ground, crackling yellow lightning at its tail. There was a smell of ozone, like the air before a storm. Denny kept his head back and watched the shuttle all through the long "nah, nah, nah" part of the song.

When Denny lowered his head, he was very surprised to find that the old chug was gone. He looked down the line of blue dots, but did not see it moving toward the air taxis. He looked down the line of green dots, but there were only three cithians pulled in under their hard black shells as they waited for the ground transport. Denny thought the chug must have gone back inside the terminal, but the glass was tinted and he could not be sure.

The old chug, it seemed, did not care much for Denny's dancing. Maybe Cousin Kettle was right.

2

At first Denny thought the chug had left no payment, but when he looked more closely, there was something new in his box. It wasn't a fat red chip, or even a slender green chip. It was a small cube, scarcely bigger than the end of Denny's thumb. Sitting in the box the cube appeared to be a pale, dusty purple, but when Denny picked it up between his thumb and first finger, little sheets of other colors ran across the sides. He had never seen anything quite like it before. It might only be a piece of trash, something the chug had left behind to mark its dislike for Denny's dance. Or maybe it was some other kind of scrip, some kind they only used on...wherever chugs came from. Whatever it was, Poppa Jam or Auntie Talla might be willing to trade for it if they knew where the little cube could be sold.

No shuttles had landed since the old chug appeared, and the long dance under the paired suns had Denny in no mood to wait for the next. Not as many shuttles seemed to come to Jukal Plex these days. Once they fell like a shower, spilling all the different kinds of people. But for cycles they had been spaced farther and farther apart. Denny frowned toward the cool glass doors of the terminal. He was thirsty. There was water at the troughs and fountains inside the port, but humans were not always welcome there. Denny might have stolen a quick swallow, or bought something from a dispenser, but some of the workers at the port made a fuss if they saw him inside and Kettle would probably give him a bad look.

Denny picked up his box, and gave a little smile at the sound of the chips clicking together. There was enough there that Denny could buy his way back to the quarter on the ground transport, and still have enough to trade Poppa Jam for a picture book or sweetpop. That was good, because otherwise Denny would have to sit outside the port and wait for the free transport that carried Kettle and the rest of the crew back to the city. Waiting for Kettle would mean sitting in the heat for another hour, which wouldn't be so bad, except Kettle would be angry to see him and make Denny beg for a ride. Denny didn't mind begging the visitors at the port so much. He did not like begging his cousin.

Denny tucked his box of credits under one arm and hurried down the green dot path toward the ground transport. When he got to the platform and saw that the cithians were still waiting for pods, he wanted to do another dance. A frustration dance. Denny wouldn't be able to ride on the next transport, because humans weren't supposed to ride in the same pod as cithians. It wasn't respectful. You could ride in the same pod as dasiks, if there were any dasiks and if the dasiks didn't press the button that simply said "No," but it was best to wait until you found an empty pod.

When the next transport showed up, Denny stood back and watched the cithians climb on. One of them was ranked high enough that its glossy black shell rose up past the top of its bowed head and the edge on either side had been carved with grooves indicating some kind of important title. Denny squinted at the little grooves, but he didn't know all the cithian ranks. He didn't know this one. The weight of the tall shell made the cithian's movements slow and ponderous. The hard tips of its four rear limbs clacked sharply as it tipped from left to right and back again. It took a pod by itself. The other two cithians shuffled into the second pod, and as they did one of them turned round and looked at Denny standing in the doorway. Right away the blunt knobs of its clangers began to rasp out a warning on the edge of its shell.

Denny lowered his head and stepped back. Humans were supposed to be grateful to the cithians. For saving them, and giving them a place to live, and stuff. Sometimes that was hard.

3

PASSDAY

On Passday, Denny got to eat. There was food on other days—orangey blocks of chez and goopey brown nutter that came in gray boxes from the Human Assistance Authority. Denny stood in the line most mornings and waited like everyone else to get his boxes from cithians who wore tight plastek gloves over their forelimbs and hard plastek masks over their faces. Sometimes there were also boxes of dry little crackers. Sometimes there was powdermilk mix for drinking. But most of the time there was just chez and nutter, nutter and chez.

Except on Passday. On Passday, Auntie Talla did Restaurant.

Auntie Talla had a place on the lower floor of an old compartment building. It had been the gather room of the building back when there were enough humans in Jukal to keep all the little rooms packed, but now it was a nothing room. Just another of those places that once had people, then didn't.

Talla and Cousin Sirah had dragged in a bunch of mismatched tables and chairs that came from empty compartments and closed stores. They had made shelves of stacked boxes, and a bar from a length of plastek with scorch marks along one end. Plates and cups and spoons had come from everywhere, no two alike.

It had been Denny's father who helped Talla build a stove out of sheet metal from a scrapped transport. They beat the metal into shape, with a firebox down below and the middle domed up like the shell on a cithians' back. Denny had been there, watching, waiting for a taste of the first meal off the new stove. He still remembered how Talla had traded with a klickik—old human junk in exchange for vegetables and spices—and how the stove had been covered deep in a layer of pop peppers mixed with loops of brown mummion and snapping strips of meat. The whole thing had smelled so good that Denny couldn't help dancing from one foot to the other while he waited for the food to finish.

His father had put a hand on Denny's shoulder and grinned down at him. "Hold your horses," he said. "We can't eat until everyone gets here."

That was the last thing Denny's father said before the blue door at the other side of the long room swung open and a handful of cithians came in, their shells rasping against the sides of the human-sized door. Behind them had come a dozen of the dasik guards. Half the humans in Jukal had been sent away on consignment that night, including Denny's father. Denny never had learned what horses were, or why he should hold them. No one who was left seemed to know.

Later, when all the humans had been hurried away and the cithians had squeezed back out through the same door they had entered, Talla had said they should eat all the food that had been cooked so it didn't go to waste. It was the only time Denny could remember having more food than he could eat. It was the only time he could remember not being hungry.

That had been two years ago. Since that night, Restaurant had been a lot less crowded. A lot less noisy. A lot less happy.

4

When Denny came through the door for Restaurant, there were only four other humans there. Auntie Talla was brushing oil across the big stove. Denny could see that there were plates of vegetables already chopped and waiting for their turn on the heat. There was some kind of meat, too. Something that Talla had bought at the market. Usually the meat came from the klickiks, in pinkish gray strips peeled off something that lived far away. Sometimes the meat was something sold by the cithians. Something that, before it was pried from its shell, looked a lot like a bigger version of the little red scuttles that prowled under boxes and in the shut-ups of Denny's compartment. Denny didn't look too closely. Usually it was better not to look at the meat until after it had been cooked.

Auntie Talla glanced up long enough to nod at Denny when he came in, but she quickly turned her attention back to her stove. She swiped at the oil as it dripped down the sides of the domed metal, pushing it back to the top with a practiced twist of her curved stick even as the oil sizzled, popped, and took on a brownish color. As soon as the oil was pushed up the metal dome of the stove, it started to ooze back down. There were little white scars all along the backs of Talla's fingers were the oil had burned her, but with fast work she could make just a spoonful of the stuff last out a meal.

Even if the oil had allowed her more time, Denny doubted Talla would have given him a greeting. She seldom said more than a few words in an evening these days and Denny could not remember the last time she had joked, or laughed, or even smiled. People had called Talla an Auntie for years, though she was barely nineteen and never anyone's mother. It was just that she was so serious, and she had watched over Cousin Sirah ever since Sirah's parents were consigned five years earlier. Young as she was, there were already lines of worry pressed into Talla's thin face, and in the last weeks Denny had noticed strands of white mingling with her dark hair.

Once this would have been about the time when everyone got together and did a jilly-ho for Talla to welcome her into the ranks of adults. There would have been a ceremony, and music, and dancing, and talk about who Talla might marry–Kettle, if it happened now, it would have to be Cousin Kettle or Cousin Haw and

Denny could not imagine Auntie Talla with Haw—and more talk about when she might have children. But all that would have to wait until Talla was consigned to somewhere else. There just weren't enough people left in Jukal Plex for a proper ceremony. It didn't seem fair that Talla was treated like an Auntie, when she never got a jilly-ho.

Denny stopped beside the stove long enough to make a show of breathing in the scents from the cooking food. It was partly just to be polite, but the green edges of the poppers were just starting to darken, and the smell was good enough that he really was tempted to reach in and steal a bite.

Auntie Talla had no trouble reading his mind. "Step back, now," she said with a wave of her oily stick. She smacked it down hard against the metal surface close to Denny's fingers. Denny snatched back his hand.

Talla would never actually hurt anyone. At least, Denny didn't think so, but he stepped back anyway. He fumbled in the pocket of his baggy shorts and came out with three green chips, leftovers from what he had earned at the spaceport. "Is this enough for Restaurant?"

"It's enough," said Talla, without bothering to look at what Denny was holding.

No matter how much or how little Denny brought, it was always enough. More than once he had come to Restaurant with nothing, and Talla had fed him just the same. Denny supposed that if he never brought in another chip, he would still not go hungry, but Denny liked to pay when he could. To get the food, Talla had to trade with cithians and dasiks and klickiks at the big market. If there were not enough chips to buy what she needed, she would have to do what others did all the time. She would have to sell some of her things to Poppa Jam.

Denny hoped Talla had enough this time.

Cousin Sirah was busy setting out dishes and cups even more mismatched than the tables they sat on. She flashed Denny a white smile as soon as she saw him.

Next to Denny, Sirah was the youngest human left in Jukal. She was not really his cousin, of course, any more that Talla was his Auntie, but for a long time now—generations, his father had said—all the adults in Jukal Plex had called each other Auntie or Uncle. Had called all the old ones Poppa or Non. Had named all the children Cousins. It was just something you did when everyone all together was not much bigger than a family.

Denny had not paid much attention to Sirah, not when there were other kids around. She had always been too serious. Too much like a little adult. Sirah had never wanted to play when she was smaller. Never wanted to dance when she was older. Sirah had never been someone to go to if you wanted fun. These last two years, there had been no one else much for Denny to talk to—no one human, at least—and he had decided that talking with Sirah was not a bad thing. Maybe that meant that

Denny was also becoming an adult. Maybe it was just that he had started to notice that Sirah was very smart, and often kind, and also kind of pretty.

"Did you see any skynx at the port?" she asked.

"I did," said Denny. He circled round the table and dropped into a chair across from Sirah. "And some dasiks, of course. And a chug. And two klickiks. "

"Klickicks?" Sirah dropped a bent froon onto a plate with a clatter. "What were they doing?"

Denny shrugged. "They were leaving. They got on the first shuttle this morning." He knew Sirah liked the klickiks, with their tall purple frills and hard red limbs. Once, one of them had come to the quarter, even come to Restaurant, and Sirah had watched it so closely she spilled a whole bowl of mummions.

Sirah finished spreading the plates across the table, took another stack in hand, and then set them back carefully. Denny saw that she was looking across the room to where a dozen or more tables had been stacked and shoved into the corner. Denny could just remember when there were enough people in the Jukal Plex to fill all those tables.

"I don't suppose..." Sirah picked up a handful of tarnished froons and started to put them beside the plates. "I don't suppose you saw any other humans at the spaceport?"

"No," said Denny. "Not today." Not on any day.

5

Denny took up the plates and helped Sirah set the tables. Mostly the plates went down in ones and twos, scattered at round tables and square tables around the big room. As few people as there were now in Jukal, they might have all sat together at just one of Restaurant's larger tables. Instead, they all sat where they used to sit when there were more cousins, more aunts and uncles, more nonnis and poppas. Restaurant used to be a place to talk, now it was a place to remember.

While they were getting things ready, Poppa Jam shuffled in and haggled with Auntie Talla. Talla always made Poppa Jam pay more for his Restaurant than the others, but that was only fair. Poppa Jam had more than any of the others. Probably more than all of them put together.

Behind him, Cousin Kettle came in, still wearing his blue cover-ups from the spaceport. He joined his mother,

Auntie Flash, who was already sitting at the corner table. Auntie Flash had been sick, and despite several visits to the Human Assistance Authority doctor, she still trembled when she walked and she talked with a strange slowness. Denny knew that Kettle had used a lot of the credits he made at the spaceport to take Auntie Flash to see a klickick doctor who was supposed to know a lot about humans. It didn't seem to have helped Auntie Flash, but knowing that he had used his credits for his mother made it hard for Denny to stay mad at Kettle.

Sharing a table with Kettle and his mother was Cousin Yulia. Yulia was actually just days younger than Auntie Talla, but no one had ever thought to call her an aunt. She had strange, pale eyes, and she always seemed so frightened. Yulia had come from Halitt Plex, the last human in that whole plex, and before she was consigned to Jukal, she had been alone for a long time. It had made her...different. She was quiet. She rarely looked at anyone. She had a big jacket, big enough that it looked like it was made for someone much larger than Yulia, and she huddled down in that jacket so much that it seemed like she wanted to disappear.

Before the rest of the remaining humans could come into the room, the other door opened—the blue door at the far side of the space.

Sirah jumped and spun around. Denny turned more slowly. Half of him was afraid that it was the patrol come to consign them all to some other place. Half of him hoped it was.

But this time, there was only a single, very large, very old cithian in the doorway. Hiser Grismalamacata Omicradiscrad, Overcontroller Human Assistance Authority, pushed his way slowly into the gather room. The big cithian had to move carefully to keep the burrs and notches of his deeply etched shell from snagging on the door. He was so old that the hinges of his shell didn't really flex well anymore, and the whole thing moved like one stiff, hard bowl. Long before he was completely in the room his broad eye pads had scanned the handful of humans. The Overcontroller held his heavy, hooked forelimbs folded across his chest as he raised a smaller mid-limb in greeting.

"Humans," he said, his voice sounding in an echoey sigh that came from all around his shell, "enjoy."

Denny wasn't sure if the Overcontroller meant to say he enjoyed being with them, or was wishing that all the humans should enjoy their meal. The older cithians became, the harder they became to understand, and Hiser Grismalamacata Omicradiscrad was about as old as a cithian ever got.

The Overcontroller finally managed to get all his bulk into the room and crossed slowly toward Auntie Talla. His hard feet clacked off the tile floor loud enough to stir echoes around the nearly empty room.

A second figure appeared in the blue doorway. This one was smaller in every way than the Overcontroller. A rounded head that was roughly the same color as the blocks of Human Assistance Authority chez looked around the edge of the opening.

Denny smiled. "Omi!" he called.

The young cithian raised the orange-red edges of its mouthparts in reply, which Denny knew–or at least thought–was the cithian equivalent of a grin. "Deee!" he shouted back. Omicradiscrad had recently been through a molt, and the softness of his shell, including the noise-plate cithians used for speaking, made it hard for him to pronounce Denny's name.

Omi waddled toward them. He was wearing a temporary shell on his back made of tough plastek, which was meant to protect his fragile body until his exoskeleton hardened after the molt. Until a few cycles before, Omi had been small, lean, and covered in a narrow shell that was a bright, orange-spotted yellow. He had looked quite unlike an adult cithian. With this latest molting Omi had taken on more of the rounded shape of the adults, though he was still only half their size and his form was still much sharper. Unlike the adult cithians, Omi wore clothing over his slow-hardening body and limbs. Enough of his head and forelimbs had hardened up that he had pulled the cloth back from those areas, but still the loose gray folds of heavy cloth completely hid the contours of his thorax and joints of his hind-limbs. Denny thought that, except for the big dark patch of his eyepads, Omi might have passed for a human with a tub strapped to his back. He'd thought that even more when Omi had been completely wrapped in cloth just after his molting, but Denny had never told this thought to Omi. He didn't want to insult his friend by comparing him to a human.

It took some time for the little cithian to reach them. Even Omi's feet were soft, and he walked with a peculiar roll from side to side. By the time he got close, Denny could see that Omi had grown after the last molt. His eyepads were now almost even with Denny's face. "Look how big you are!" said Denny. He shook his head. "Another molt or two, and you'll be an adult."

"Yes, yes," Omi agreed. His voice sounded funnier than usual as it bounced from the plastic shell. "One or uuoo...or two."

Omi joined Denny and Cousin Sirah at a small table. They talked and waited while Talla served the Overcontroller and the rest of the humans. At the far end of the room, old Nonni Hacci came in. Shortly after that, Auntie Yue and Auntie Fro joined her at a table. Everyone was there but Poppa Gow, but his absence wasn't unusual. Poppa Gow had been sick for a long time, and he needed a wheeled chair to get around. Denny would take some Restaurant to Poppa Gow later. He didn't mind. He liked seeing all the things that Poppa Gow kept in his compartment.

Denny offered Omi some of his food, but Omi's mouthparts were still too soft to eat most of it. At the moment, Omi could only drink liquids. It would be another cycle before he could eat anything he wanted.

Before the last molt, Omi had spent a lot of time hanging around the human quarter. He was the only cithian who seemed to care about human music, or listening to the old stories. On this visit, Omi told them that, now that he was getting close to his final molting, he would have to spend more time following Overcontroller Hiser. There would be no more time for things like music and games. No time for silly human stories.

Omi was the Overcontroller's second. Cithians didn't have families like humans. Most of them had no idea who their parents were. They thought the way humans put so much time into thinking about family was rather strange. It was just genes. Only those cithians who had done something important were allowed to create, not a child, but a copy of themselves. You could tell that Overcontroller Hiser was a very important cithian, because he had not one copy, but two. Omi was the new one. The first copy, Grismalamacata, had been made years ago. Denny had never seen him, but he'd heard that Grismalamacata already had a copy of his own. Some of the most famous cithians were copies of copies of copies.

"One day you'll be the Overcontroller," said Denny, thinking of when Omi replaced Hiser, "and you'll be the one who tells us what to do."

Omi slurped at a cup of water and bobbed his head. "I will know oow, 'ut...but then ii...it will be uuoo laa. Too late."

Denny took a second to work this out. "Too late for what?"

The flat black eyepads studied Denny. "You..." Omi stopped and spoke more slowly, forming the Xetosh words as carefully as he could. "You doo...don't know?"

Denny glanced over at Cousin Sirah. She only looked back at him and shook her head. "I guess I don't," he said.

"You aaa...all you humaa...you all ee..." Omi tried again. "You all humans are leaving soon," he said. "You're all being consigned." Then his mouthparts went up again in that cithian smile.

6

SKIMSDAY

On Skimsday, Denny went shopping. He stopped first for his nutter and chez, which didn't take too long. One thing about there not being many humans left in the plex was that the lines were always short. He got his food, ate most of it sitting on the broken pavement in the dim sunshine, and still had the whole day ahead.

The dull red sun was still just starting its long roll around the Skimsday sky when Denny knocked on the corrugated metal door of Poppa Jam's Porium. The Porium was at the center of a long block of small buildings with slide up front doors and narrow windows. Denny could just remember when all the buildings had been stores. Rasha's bakery, and Wallin's woodstuff, and Luxa's. Denny couldn't remember what Luxa had sold.

It didn't matter anyway. The others were gone. Now the only store left was Poppa Jam's.

The tall door rolled up, and Jam looked out. For just a moment, he looked very old, and a bit confused, with his spotted bald head and his heavy gray brows, then he saw Denny and he rolled his yellowy eyes. "It's barely light," he said. "What are you doing here so early?"

"It's Skimsday," said Denny with a shrug. "This is about as light as it gets."

"Is it?" Poppa Jam leaned past Denny and looked up at the scarlet-tinged sky. "Then I guess I'm open." He turned his back on a Denny and shuffled off into the cluttered aisles of the store.

Denny followed him under the hanging door. The walls on either side had been knocked down, none too neatly, expanding Poppa Jam's space into the empty shops on either side. Once, the Porium had been filled mostly with things that come from the cithians or the skynx, things that the humans wanted to buy. There were still a few things like that here and there. Sets of glossy, colorful bowls that were made by the chugs. A curling horn that had come from some beast of from the skynx home planet. A pair of heavy plastek molting shells like the one Omi had worn at Restaurant. Thick cithian cloth so stiff that any shirt made of it was guaranteed to rub a human raw. To Denny, all that stuff looked like plain old junk.

Most of Poppa Jam's Porium was the other way around. Now most of the dusty shelves and stacked corners were filled with things that used to be in the compartments and gather rooms of the humans, and most of the customers were cithians, or skynx, or chugs who came in to buy these human left overs. Denny had even seen a pair of lesser dasiks carrying away an orangey couch.

"So, you come to sell me something?" Poppa Jam said without bothering to turn around. "Finally going to give up one of those ugly lumps your father left behind?"

"I'm buying," said Denny. He stopped near the counter, where there were still a handful of klickick picture books and a bin of sweetpops. Denny had never been sure who made the sweetpops. Probably not the cithians. None of their food ever tasted right to Denny. Surely not the skynx. Skynx food was...well, it was nothing that a human would try twice. Poppa Jam watched Denny flip through the books for a moment, then just shook his head and shuffled away.

Denny saw someone else enter the Porium. He turned to see that it was Cousin Yulia. As usual, Yulia was wearing her big jacket, which seemed much too warm for Jukal, but then Yulia had come from Halitt Plex, where it was supposed to be a much colder place, even on Whetsday. Maybe Yulia still carried some of that cold with her.

Denny held up the picture book to show Yulia, but she wasn't looking his way. She fingered a roll of the rough cithian cloth, and then walked on and disappeared among the shelves.

A moment later there was a thump from the corner of the big room and Cousin Haw came in. Haw worked for Poppa Jam, and Denny rarely saw him anywhere but the Porium. He seemed to have two jobs, carrying things and looking mean. He was pretty good at both of them. It helped that Haw was the biggest human in Jukal. In fact, Denny thought if you added all the other humans left in the quarter together, including Cousin Kettle, who was pretty big on his own, you just might have enough to make one Cousin Haw.

Cousin Haw was eating from a gray carton of nutter, digging out mouthfuls of the stuff with a flat plastic froon. He spotted Denny by the counter and angled his way. "You finally going to sell your dad's junk?" Haw said.

"No." Denny grabbed up a yellowish sweetpop and not one, but two of the picture books.

The first book was tattered at one corner, and when Denny looked inside it was clear that all the images had degraded to bits of digital noise. In some of them, he could just make out the shadows of a moving...skynx? klickik? But really, the silent, messy pages were ruined.

The cover of the second book came alive at his touch. The material of the cover looked like the same water-stained brown paper as the first, but this time the big green form of a planet or moon rolled smoothly into view as soon as Denny's finger settled onto the page. The rest of the green form trailed slowly around the edge of the book, covered with spirals of cloud and scattered circles of blue marking craters filled with water. As Denny continued to watch, the darting shape of a sleek, silvery spaceship came into view. The world grew even larger as the spaceship homed in. There was a momentary stutter and the image turned pale–few of the old things in the Porium worked perfectly–but then it picked up again, and the ship spiraled down to disappear against the deep green side of the little world.

When Denny peeked inside, he was surprised to see that several of the other pages were also working. This was a good one. An amazing one, really. He had never seen a book in Jam's store where more than a few of the images still moved. He could even hear the tiny squeak of voices coming up from the pages as he flipped to the heart of the book. He ran his thumb along the side and the voices grew louder. This book worked. Maybe all the way through.

"I'll take this," he said, waving the floppy pages of the book in the air and speaking loudly so Poppa Jam would hear.

Haw only snorted at his choice and spooned in more of his nutter. Poppa Jam took a while returning from whatever he was doing in the back. When he saw the book in Denny's hand, his shaggy brows went up. "That's a good one. You got credits?"

Denny dipped into his pocket, producing a pair of green chips.

Jam shook his head. "Take a lot more than that," he said.

"Well..." Denny felt carefully in his pocket and found the edge of a fat red chip. He added it to the stack on the counter.

Poppa Jam only shook his head again. "Still not enough." He tugged the book from Denny's fingers and thumbed through its pages. "Book like this, perfect condition..."

"It's not..."

"Near perfect condition," said Poppa Jam. He closed the book and put it on the counter. "Book like this is worth at least three red."

"Three red!"

"At least."

Denny dug deep. With everything, he had barely two red, and if he gave all of that to Poppa Jam, there would be nothing else for the rest of the week. He'd have to go back to dance at the spaceport before next Restaurant if he wanted to pay for his food.

Before Denny could make another offer, a tall figure appeared at the shop door. It was a dasik–a *greater* dasik–with the long spines on its back and even longer teeth lapping the sides of its mouth. Poppa Jam at once forgot about Denny and hustled over to great his new customer. He said something to the tall creature that Denny couldn't hear, and in response the dasik pressed the button that said "Show me." Poppa Jam lead the dasik back into the shelves.

The book was still sitting on the counter, and Danny decided this might be a good time to simply read it. Poppa Jam got pretty upset sometimes if he thought Denny was getting too much out of a book without paying for it, but with the dasik here, Jam wasn't likely to notice. Besides, Denny didn't have three reds.

He opened the book to the first page. The silver spaceship was just landing on the surface of the green, vine-tangled planet. Denny had expected the ship to be crewed by klickiks, but instead a trio of tiny figures in white slid down the ramp, moving quickly on their little legs. Something, something big and dark, moved in the vines. One of the figures raised an instrument in the curl of its tail and the book gave a tiny squeak. Denny reached up to slide his hand over the page in the way that would make the book louder.

Cousin Haw's big hand came down on Denny's with enough force to make him jerk in pain. "No reading in the store," said Haw.

Denny tried to pull his hand free, but Haw pressed down, grinding his fingers into the counter. "You're going to hurt the book," Denny said through clenched teeth.

For a moment, Haw actually smiled, but after a bit he raised his heavy hand. "Wouldn't want to hurt...the book," he said.

Poppa Jam emerged from the back of the store, a deep scowl on his face, and Denny saw Cousin Yulia peek out for a moment around the end of a sagging shelf before she returned to her own shopping.

"What's going on up here," Jam said in a fierce whisper. "Can't you see we have a customer?"

Denny flexed his aching fingers. "I still want the book."

"Do you have three red? Because if you don't..."

A sudden thought struck Denny. He thrust his aching hand into his pocket and came out with the glossy little cube that the chug had dropped into his tray. "I have this."

"What is it?" Poppa Jam stepped closer, leaning down to take a closer look. Immediately, his eyes went wide. He turned his head, looking back over his shoulder at where the greater dasik was still rummaging through the store. "Put it away," Jam said, his voice dropping back to a whisper. "Put it away now."

Denny look at him in surprise. "Why?"

"Please assist," said the voice of the dasik's talk button from the back of the store.

Poppa Jam stepped around, putting himself between Denny and the dasik, then made another quick look over his shoulder. "You're not supposed to have that."

"Why not?"

"Because–"

"Please assist," said the talk button again, this time from somewhere closer.

Poppa Jam looked as if someone was squashing <u>his</u> fingers. "Take it out of here," he said quickly. "Take it to old Loma. She can tell you about it. Just take it out of here." Then Poppa Jam turned away and shuffled toward the back of the store just about as fast as Denny had ever seen him move.

Denny turned the cube between his fingers, watching the colors play over the flat sides. He wondered what there could be about something so small that made Poppa Jam so upset.

A heavy hand came down on Denny's shoulder. "You heard him. Get moving."

"I'm going." Denny cast one more look toward the book that was still spread open on the counter. The little figures in white suits were fighting with something big and scary. It looked like a very interesting story.

But Denny also had something interesting to do. He shoved the cube safely back into his pocket and left the Porium. From somewhere back in the store, he heard the dasik's talk button say "Yes, I will take all of it."

7

Cousin Kettle grabbed Denny coming out of the Porium, and made him come back to the compartment building to help with moving furniture down from the level where Kettle and Auntie Flash made their home. Like many of the compartments, Kettle's place was tiny and cramped. He and his mother might have taken over the whole floor. Except for Cousin Yulia, who lived in another little compartment right below them, there was not another human within a dozen levels. But like so many of the humans remaining in Jukal Plex, Kettle and Flash had not spread out when their neighbors were consigned to some other place. Some people had tried it. Poppa Gow had turned a whole floor into his compartment. But spreading out only seemed to make most folks feel even more alone than they did in their little places. Some people even said the old, empty apartments were haunted. Denny didn't believe that, but he also didn't like to go into the places where families had come and gone. It was sad.

Kettle drummed his fingers across the top of an old closetbox as they waited for the lift down to the gather room. "You should go through your own stuff," he said to Denny. "Time to clear everything out and get ready to leave."

Denny only shrugged. "Why?"

"Because Poppa Jam will pay for it." The whistle sounded and Kettle tipped the box over so that he and Denny could wrestle it onto the platform. "Because it'll be a whole lot easier to carry a handful of credits instead of a bunch of junk when the authority comes to consign us all."

"Someone is always saying we're going to leave soon." Denny sat down his end of the box as the lift began to move down. "If I cleaned out things every time, I'd have been sitting on the floor for the last cycle."

"It's a lot different when one of them says it instead of one of us," replied Kettle. "You know the old saying about consignment—you can't take it with you." Which was true enough. Most of the time, people got no warning when consignment really came. You got consigned with clothes on your back and nothing else.

By the time Denny was through helping Kettle, the scarlet sky of Skimsday had settled into a deep purple. There were some light clouds crossing the sky that were lit more by reflections from the plex than they were by the pair of faint stars. Sometimes, if you looked very carefully right about the time that Skimsday turned into Dimsday, out of the corner of your eye, you could even catch a glimpse of stars.

Denny rode the lift back to his own home, eight levels up from the gather room, and slipped into the compartment. No one else had been there in a long time, almost two years, and Kettle would have been surprised if he could actually see inside. The truth was, Denny had already sold off nearly every stick of furniture, every lamp, every knick-knack, doodad, and geegaw his family had picked up while living in Jukal Plex. He'd sold them to pay for Restaurant on those days when dancing hadn't gotten any chips and he was too embarrassed to go to Talla empty handed. He'd sold them for when Auntie Flash got sick, and everyone had chipped in to help. He'd sold them for when he outgrew his shoes and Poppa Jam charged way too much for new ones. He'd even sold things to pay for picture books and sweetpops, both because he liked them, and because it was important that nobody understood just how little he had left.

He'd sold almost everything. The beds. The chairs. Even most of the clothes and plates. He'd sold everything but the things his father made.

Denny's father hadn't just known how to beat metal into a stove. He'd known how to twist it, stretch it, cut it, shape it, until it formed things that were more than just useful. He'd known how to make things that people didn't have a name for, but which all people–humans and chugs and klickiks and even cithians–had a need.

In the center of the floor in Denny's compartment, there was a small figure made of metal. It wasn't the most detailed of the things his father had made, and it was far from the largest, but Denny gave it a big space in the room. It looked like a man, or maybe a boy. It looked sort of like he was dancing. It looked sort of like he was shaking his fists at the sky.

Denny laid down next to the statue and fell asleep on the hard floor.

8

DIMSDAY

On Dimsday, Denny took a walk. In the stuttering gray-blue light of Dimsday morning, Denny left the compartment building and hurried down the central street that ran through the human quarter. The street had no actual name, just a number in the massive snarl of Jukal Plex, but someone—someone long ago—had put up a sign that said Oak Street. Denny had no idea what the sign meant.

At the end of the narrow street, Denny passed between the two low, blocky buildings that guarded the edge of the quarter. The old gate and cutwires were gone, but you could still see the heavy posts where they had once been bolted to the walls. In the half-light, with the bright point of the tiny blue sun still just about to rise, everything seemed, not just dim and shadowy, but actually made of shadows. Like a dream, though not an especially good one.

Just outside the quarter were the empty sleeping stadium where the staff of the Human Assistance Authority had lived, and the even larger buildings where humans had been tested and examined when they were being brought into Jukal Plex. Nearly all of the buildings were empty now. The only lights were around the smaller building where the Overcontroller, Omi, and the few remaining guards were sleeping.

Passing through all the long, empty spaces, Denny wondered what it had been like when these buildings had been filled with people coming in from other places. Had they been excited to be there? Had they been worried? A few people had come to Jukal in the last few years, but only a handful, and most of those had already been consigned again somewhere else. Denny tried to peek into one of the silent halls, but there was nothing to see but darkness. It must have been very different back when there were hundreds, or even thousands, of humans coming here. Everything crowded and noisy and busy. Maybe it would be like that again, once they were consigned to somewhere else.

Denny came out into Jukal and stayed on the perimeter of the great plex, so most of the largest buildings were still some ways off in the distance, looming up out of the darkness. Even though it was almost all the way on the far side of the city, the

Cataclysm stood higher than everything else. There was a gap between the tall white spike and the rest of the plex. Denny knew there was a wall between it and the other buildings, though he had never been close enough to see it.

The cithians had tried to do something special at the Cataclysm. Make some kind of power plant said some of the old stories. Build too high, said another–though that didn't make sense to Denny, since shuttles went higher every day. Whatever had happened, it was bad, and now anyone who got too close to the Cataclysm would die. Which seemed like a good reason to stay far away.

The sections of the plex where Denny traveled were typical for the edges of Jukal. There were the big stadiums where most of the cithians slept away Dimsday, nestled in piles with little regard for rank. Cithians didn't have family homes–didn't really have families–so the arrangement kind of made sense, though Denny was glad that humans didn't live that way. He wouldn't have liked listening to Poppa Jam snore. Around these sleeping domes were domed buildings for storage and tall cubes where the cithians did...whatever it was that most cithians did for most of the cycle. Despite the new rules, humans still weren't allowed in most of the cithian buildings. The Overcontroller said it was for their own safety. Cithian workers had to concentrate on their work. They couldn't be looking out for foolish, careless, easily injured humans.

Each grouping of buildings was connected to the rest by both streets and by the ground transport. Some were even hooked together by the tall sky transports or by air taxis. Humans weren't allowed on either of those. Denny might have taken the ground transport, but sometimes the pods weren't all running on Dimsday, and he didn't know how to give directions to where he was going. And he was almost out of credits. So he just kept walking.

On most days, the streets between the buildings would have been crowded with cithians, and Denny would have spent much of his time just staying out of their way, but this was Dimsday. On Dimsday, most cithians stayed in the stadiums, resting during the near darkness. Now just about the only cithians he saw were the darting yellow shapes of the very young, and those like Omi, fresh off a molt, with the plastic shells on their backs and their soft bodies covered in cloth. The moltlings moved around slowly, clumsily, unable to rest with the other cithians until their new shells had at least started to harden. They really couldn't do much, not even make a warning rumble, but Denny stayed away from them as much as he could.

He made his way down the nearly empty streets, being careful to cross when he had to, dodging around the occasional road ferry, giving as much room to the few cithians he met as he could. Even so, more than one cithian rumbled at Denny, thumping their clangers against their shells in a sound that was half threat, half alarm. Twice Denny was stopped by cithians who had the red slash of the Jukal Plex Legal Authority striped across their shells. One of these made Denny empty his backpack, and spilled half his water before accepting that it was just water. Fortunately, Denny still had the purple cube in his pocket, and no one found it.

Slowly the flickering light of the blue sun wheeled around the perimeter of the sky. The winds that sliced in along the curving streets were actually chilly enough to make Denny shiver. He kind of wished now that he had a big jacket, like Yulia. He also wished there was a way to capture some of that coolness and keep it with him. He would be happy to have it when Whetsday swung around again.

Denny was very tired and thirsty by the time he caught sight of the black lake glimmering in the half-light. A curve of land swept out into the black lake, and on the end of this curve was a series of very small buildings made of stone that matched the shimmer of the sky. There were lights out there in pale pink and faded green, lights that were reflected into smears on the dark waters. Denny turned off the broad road and walked through the more twisty paths that lead out to the skynx community.

Unlike the cithians, the skynx kept small, neat little houses that were as close to the water as they could get. Those that were not directly against the black lake were raised up a bit so that those inside could see down to the waters. As far as Denny could tell, none of the homes was more than a few steps from the shore. The skynx liked water.

As Denny got closer, he could see that some of the skynx were out and moving between the homes. Even more of them were actually in the waters of the lake. The little paddles that lined the sides of the skynx' flexible bodies seemed as good at moving them around in water as they were on land. Under the faint bluish light of Dimsday, the skynx' red-brown bodies were as black as the waters of the little lake, but they moved fast enough to carve curling wakes in the still water. Several times Denny saw a skynx throw itself completely free of the water, twist, glistening, through the air, and come back to the lake with only the slightest splash. Wether it was for a purpose or just for fun, Denny couldn't say. Maybe this was skynx dancing.

The first of the skynx that Denny encountered on the street ignored him. They slipped around him on their long, low bodies, moving past as if he was just another obstacle. It wasn't until he stood in the center of the path and called out "'Scuse me" that one of the skynx actually stopped and turned his way.

The skynx raised its head until it was nearly as tall as Denny. "Yes?" it asked. It had the same fast, chirpy voice as every other skynx Denny had ever met.

"I'm looking for a human."

"Human?" A ripple moved through the paddles at the front of the skynx' long body. "They are there," it said, shaping its front paddles into an arrow that pointed back the way Denny had come.

"Not the human quarter," said Denny. "Just one. Old Loma."

In response, the skynx dropped back to its paddles and took off along the path at such a pace that Denny had to run to keep up.

Two years before, when the Human Assistance Authority had consigned Denny's father and so many others from Jukal off to new locations, Overcontroller Hiser had announced that the rules which said that humans had to stay in the quarter were being relaxed. It was a big surprise to the few humans left. From now on, humans would be allowed to travel around the city as they pleased, so long as they didn't get on any of the transports leaving Jukal Plex. And, of course, so long as they showed the proper respect to their cithian hosts. And stayed away from cithian buildings, and cithian transports, and especially the Cataclysm.

Most humans had been excited to get a chance to see more of the great city where generations of humans had lived, but never really been a part. Denny still liked to visit the spaceport, and watch the many different peoples who visited the markets and squares near the center of the city. Auntie Talla also got out into the city, shopping for food at the market, and trading things she cooked. A few others, like Kettle, had even gotten jobs out among the citizens of Jukal. But many of the humans had found that giving the cithians proper respect meant always waiting for an empty transport or walking in a hot street on Whetsday so cithians could enjoy the shade. That made traveling around the city less pleasant. Many had found it was easier to just stay in the quarter.

When it came to places to live, even though the authority would now allow them to travel to most areas, the humans still lived in the quarter. All but one.

Denny was just about to decide that the skynx he was following didn't really know Old Loma and wasn't taking him anywhere in particular, when the low figure stopped at the front of one of the tiny houses. "The human is here," it said. Then it left, moving faster than ever.

From what Denny could see, the house looked like the other houses. Same low doors. Same pink and green lights. Same walls made from stone that was, close up, actually more like melted glass. It didn't look like a human place.

Even so, he went to the small door at the corner and rapped against it with his knuckles. It turned out that the door was more like a thick curtain, changing Denny's knocks into soft thumps. He rapped again at the frame. "Old Loma?" he said. "Are you here?"

The door curtain was suddenly swept aside. The woman on the other side was short, short enough that the skynx' door seemed well suited to her. She wore a loose robe crossed by dark bands, and her hair was a thin, fly-away tangle of white puffs. Her eyes stared at Denny with an expression that seemed more angry than surprised.

"Old Loma, I'm..."

"You're Carrel's boy," she said, cutting him off. She leaned out the door for a moment and looked along the dimly-lit path behind Denny. "You alone?"

"Yes, I..."

Loma held the door open wider. "Get in here," she said. "Quickly."

Denny stepped into the house, and the door immediately fell back into place. For a moment, the room was truly dark, and Denny saw nothing but nothing. Then a light flashed on. Like some of the lights outside, it had a pinkish tone. The room it revealed was small, low-ceilinged, and cramped from top to bottom with shelves, papers, and small boxes that Denny didn't recognize.

Old Loma stepped around him. She looked older than Denny remembered from the last time she had been in the quarter. He supposed she was older. There were new creases in the skin of her face, and the whites of her eyes had taken on a yellow tint that did nothing to soften her expression. "What are you doing here, Carrel's boy?"

"I..." Denny stopped and cleared his throat. "Old Loma, I'm here to..."

"Don't call me that," she said, cutting him off again. "I feel old enough without you reminding me."

"Nonni Loma?"

"Just Loma will do," Loma said. She walked slowly around Denny. "You've grown."

Denny shrugged. "You've been gone."

9

Denny took a careful sip of the water Loma had given him. "Is this from the lake?" he asked.

Loma gave a snort. "I hope not." She leaned toward one of the room's small windows and pushed aside a curtain. For just a moment, Denny could see the skynx sliding across the inky water. "There are so many metals in that water, that a glass of it would likely be the last thing you ever drank."

"Doesn't it bother the skynx?"

"Nah. They like it that way." Loma let the curtain close and crossed the room to settle herself on a low pillow that seemed to be the closest thing in the room to a chair. She pushed a few of the things that Denny thought were small boxes out of her way, and he was surprised to see that the boxes weren't boxes at all. They had pages, like a picture book, though he didn't see any pictures. Loma stared up at Denny, her dark eyes shining from the deep folds of her face. "Now tell me. What made you take such a long hike?"

Denny had thought so much about finding his way to Loma, that he had forgotten to put much thought into what he might say when he found her. "I was dancing," he began, "and there was a chug..." He fished into his pocket. "It gave me this."

Loma leaned toward him, her attention fixed on Denny's hand as he pulled out the purple cube. Her eyes went wide and she let out a low sound. "Uhhhh." She pushed down at his hand and looked up quickly at both the door and the window. She started to reach for the cube, then stopped.

Loma climbed up from her cushion and went back to the door. She tied a rope from the edge of the curtain to the wall, then tested the curtain with a tug. It didn't open. Loma nodded and rubbed her hands against her robe at her hips, as if she were wiping dirt from her hands. Or sweat.

"All right," she said. "Give it here."

Denny hadn't thought much about the cube at first, and had been willing to trade it to Poppa Jam for a picture book, but seeing how much Loma reacted to the little thing made him reluctant I hand it over.

Loma seemed almost as reluctant to take it, but after a moment her fingers darted to Denny's palm and she lifted the small, purplish object. She held it in front of her face. Then she walked closer to one of the pink lights and turned the cube back in forth in front of the glow. Once again, Denny could see how all the different colors came and went in the light. "You're not supposed to have this," said Loma. "Where did you get it?"

Denny hesitated for a moment, trying to think of what to say, but if he was going to get in trouble for having this thing, he guessed he was already in trouble. He told Loma about going to the spaceport, and how the chug had watched him, and about singing Judy. "When I was done, chug gave it to me. Is it... dangerous?"

"Dangerous?" Loma gave a little snort, then did it again. It took Denny a moment to think she might actually be laughing. "Yah. It could be dangerous. For you...and for others." She flipped the cube over in her fingers for a few seconds longer, then turned and held it up where Denny could see the color-slick sides. "It's a memory."

A memory. Denny looked down at the shiny surface of the little box. He could remember playing with the other children in the street outside the food dispersal center. He could remember his father working with Auntie Talla to pound out the stove. He could remember the awful feeling as his father was dragged out of the gather room for consignment. "Memories are just in your head," he said.

"Nah. This isn't that kind of memory," said Loma. Again she looked toward the door, and she lowered her voice so that Denny had to strain to hear her. "It's for a maton. This cube that tells them how to work."

Denny turned the idea over in his mind. He'd seen simple matons. Cithians sometimes carried them around, and he knew they used them for whatever it was they did in those buildings humans never entered. Even the buttons that talked for the dasiks were a kind of maton. But there were other kinds of matons, as well. Ones that were supposed to be seriously bad. If you saw anything that you thought might be a maton, you were supposed to tell someone, and humans were not supposed to touch them. Not ever.

"Matons are dangerous," said Denny. "If you touch one..."

"If you touch one, what happens?"

"You can die. Or at least get really sick."

The woman looked thoughtful. "Yah... Well, maybe. Maybe not." She rolled the small cube between her fingers. "I don't have a maton—restricted technology, no humans allowed—but I have something else." She turned away from Denny and went to one corner of the room where a stack of the little no-pictures books were heaped nearly waist high. From the top of the stack, she took an off-white something that was about the same size as one of the books, but had the hard gleam of metal or plastic. "I'm not really supposed to have even this," she said, stroking one thing finger along the top of the little device. "But some of the skynx think it's funny to give me things."

She touched the thing somewhere on its side, and a small opening appeared at the top. She tipped it slightly, and showed Denny that there was something inside. He stepped closer. It was another cube. As far as he could tell, it was the same size as the one the chug had given him, only this one was a pale blue instead of purple.

Loma touched another spot on the device, and at once a loud sound began. Denny jumped back, bumped against another stack of the books, and nearly fell, before he realized that the device was making music.

Sometimes, especially when they were having Restaurant, some of the people back in the quarter liked to make music. Cousin Kettle had an instrument, a string-jo, that had come from his father, or his father's father, or somebody before that, and he knew how to make the twangs and strums that went with several songs. Poppa Jam would beat his hands against the table in time to Kettle's playing, and if she was in a good mood, Auntie Talla would sing. Sometimes even Cousin Yulia would forget her fear long enough to sing along. Yulia could sing really well.

But even the best music Denny had ever heard in Restaurant was nothing like this. This was music made of every kind of sound, all playing at once, and it wasn't just noise. It was fire and light. It was metal and air. It was perfect.

Loma touched the little device again and the music stopped. "Tchaikovsky," she said.

Denny realized that he had been holding his breath. He sucked in some air and tried to get his tongue around the word that Loma has said, but it was too complicated. "What's that?"

"It's..." Loma looked thoughtful for a moment, then gave another of her snorty laughs. "I don't know. Something from the skynx, I think."

"Is that their kind of music?" Denny had been told that the skynx could dance. If this was what their music was like, he could only imagine what it would be like to see them dance.

"Maybe." Loma tilted the device to the side and the pale blue cube spilled out. She caught it and put it with a small group of others that Denny hadn't noticed until that moment. Then she took the purple cube he had brought and put it inside. "I've only seen something like this once before, and the memory won't work here like it would in a maton, but there may be something."

She pressed the side of the device. A light appeared in the center of the room

I O

SMALLPOX

Smallpox was a disease. It was one of the most infectious diseases ever encountered. Sometimes it was called just "pox," sometimes it was called "red plague."

If you caught the disease, your body would be covered by horrible, painful blisters; blisters that crowded every inch of your skin from your feet to your head. Blisters on the palms of your hands and the tips of your fingers. Blisters on every inch of your face. Blisters on your lips. Blisters on your eyelids. Blisters in your ears. Blisters on your tongue.

If you lived through the disease, you would be covered with disfiguring scars for the rest of your life. You might also be blind. You might find that your hands and feet ached terribly all your life. You might be crippled. You might be crazy.

The people who were scarred, and blind, and crippled, and crazy were the lucky ones. Many people did not live through the disease. Smallpox killed about one third of all the people infected. It killed about two thirds of children. Year after year, for hundreds of years, smallpox killed people by the hundreds of thousands. In bad years it killed millions.

Finally, after smallpox had killed over half a billion people, it was discovered that there were ways to control the disease. All the people worked together to stop smallpox, and in an amazingly short time this disease that had killed people for centuries and millennia, was gone.

But it wasn't completely gone.

In a few places, people kept small containers with samples of the disease. They knew it was dangerous. Sometimes a little of the disease would get out, and sometimes people would die.

Still, they kept it because they were worried. They kept it because they thought that somewhere out there in the wild, in some place they hadn't looked, smallpox might still be around. They worried that if they destroyed their last samples, they might not understand the disease if they needed to fight smallpox again.

Slowly, first in one place and then the next, they destroyed what was left of smallpox. Finally, there was only a single tiny test tube left of this disease that had killed so many, scarred so many, left so many in misery.

And when the people decided that it was too dangerous to keep that last little tube, they destroyed it too.

Then they celebrated, because the terrible pox, the red plague, the horror of so many lifetimes, was gone.

II

TOLLSDAY

On Tollsday, Denny read a book. He could already read enough Xetosh to understand street signs and get by at the spaceport. Like everyone, he certainly knew the cluster of symbols that meant No Humans Allowed. Learning that much made life a lot less painful.

Really, he had never learned much more than was needed to find his way back to the quarter by ground transport, and what he needed to stay out of the cithians' way. Even the picture books he bought from Poppa Jam rarely had more than a few words, and if you paid attention, you could understand the story without even reading them. Denny could have learned more, but, well...it wasn't like teaching humans to read was illegal, not really. It was just pointless. Everybody knew that. After all, the cithians had done lots of tests to show that humans were inferior at math, at reasoning, at everything that really mattered. No one was ever going to hire a human as a technician, much less an engineer. Humans were good for doing what they were told. Or maybe for dancing. So for humans, reading just wasn't important.

Denny looked over to the corner of the room, where Loma was still sleeping on her cushion. The old woman had one of the no-picture books under her head for a pillow, and another one close to her hand.

On the floor next to her was the small metal device that still held Denny's cube. As soon as Loma had pressed the spot on the device that made it go, there had been a light, then a voice had started speaking, then pictures had appeared in the middle of the small room. The voice told the story of a horrible disease. The pictures showed humans so covered with blisters that it was hard to tell they were humans. If Denny had seen one of them when he was at the spaceport, he might have thought they were from some distant planet. More distant than poor old Earth.

Denny sort of wished he had never seen it.

He went to the nearest window and raised the curtain with one finger. Outside the sky had gone a hard gray and the tiny blue sun was raising eye-searing glints from the edges of the glassy houses. Denny didn't see any skynx, but back at the end of the little strip of land, road ferries were moving in slow procession. Tollsday was a workday for the cithians.

Denny let the curtain close and rubbed his eyes. He picked up one of the books from a heap and stared at it. There was no animation. No sound or music. There were only a handful of words on the cover. Denny could make out "The" and "Count" and "by." The rest were words he didn't know. Even sounding out the letters didn't help. He flipped through the pages. Just words, words, and more words. He put a finger to a page. "All human..." He began, speaking softly, but the next word was one that hadn't been in any of his picture books, or on a street sign. "All human wiss...."

"All human wisdom is contained in these two words—wait and hope," Loma said from the floor. She rolled over and sat, rubbing at her flyaway hair.

Denny looked at the words. Yes, that was what it said, as best he could tell. "Do you know all these books?"

"Yah. Some better than others," said Loma. She put her hands against the floor and slowly pressed herself to her feet. "There's a lot of things in that book you're holding about patience. About making plans over a long time, and about getting justice." She took the book from Denny's hands. "I'd like to think there's some truth to those things, but I don't know anymore."

Denny pointed to the device on the floor. "Why did it show us those things?" He asked. "About that disease?"

Loma put the book back on top of the nearest heap. "It only showed us what was in the memory," she said, "and only part of that. A memory like this, it has more in it than all these books." She waved a thin hand around the room. "And it can do more than just show you pictures and words."

"Can we see the rest?" asked Denny.

"Nah. Not with this." Loma picked up the little device from the floor and tipped it on its side. The little cube that was a memory fell out into her hand. "To see what's in here, you still need a maton."

"But you don't have one."

"I don't," said Loma. She held the cube out to Denny. "I'm not even supposed to have the books and player."

Denny took the memory, looked for a moment at its gleaming sides, and shoved it deep into his pocket. "I never saw books like this. Who made them?"

For the first time, Loma smiled. "Humans." She lifted a thin volume from the floor and ran her hands over it. Denny could hear the soft noise of her dry palms moving over the cover. "Every one of them was written by humans, for humans, long ago." She gave the book a look that had the same kind of affection Denny had sometimes seen Auntie Talla show toward Cousin Sirah. Then Loma's expression changed and she tossed the book away without even looking at where it landed. "So naturally, I got them from the skynx." She went to the window again, lifting the curtain enough to let in the dazzling blue light of the new day. 'If you want to know what humans made, you have to ask some other people."

Denny thought of asking why the skynx would have all these human books, but he guessed he wasn't really surprised. All his life he'd watched humans trading away the little that they had for a bit of food, a moment of comfort.

He put his hand in his pocket and fingered the sharp edges of the memory. "Does someone else have a maton?" he asked. "Would the skynx..."

"Nah," Loma said sharply. "Don't say anything to the skynx about a maton. Or about a memory." She looked around again, as if worried that a skynx might have come into the room while she wasn't looking. "And be sure you don't let the cithians find out. Don't say anything to anyone. If they found out a human has been handling a memory..." Loma gave a snort, but this time it sounded less like laughing. "We'd both be consigned by the end of the day."

"Everyone is getting consigned soon anyway."

Loma took a step toward him and looked hard into his face. "What?"

"Omi, I mean, one of the cithians, he said that all the rest of the humans were going to be consigned soon." Denny shrugged. "Maybe I should just wait till then before we try to find a maton."

The idea that they were going to be consigned had seemed half-frightening and half-hopeful to Denny. After all, they were bound to be taken somewhere with more people than the pitiful few left in Jukal. There would probably be reunions. He might not see his father, that was too much to hope for, but *someone* would find a lost parent, or child, or at least a friend.

Only Loma seemed to think the idea that the last humans in Jukal were about to be consigned was all bad. Denny could see it just looking at the tight expression on the old woman's face. At the deepening of the nest of lines around her eyes. Loma thought that this was a horrible idea.

"Don't," she said. Her hand went again to the fine tufts of her hair. "Don't wait for anything. If you're—"

Before she could finish, there was a drumming sound from the door. Loma stepped quickly to loose the cord that held the curtain closed. She had barely moved the curtain itself when a skynx paddled its way into the room.

Denny had seen many skynx at the spaceport, and of course he'd seen the swimmers in the lake, but for all that he might as well have seen only one. He thought that some were larger than others, but there no markings that he could see. No difference in the color, or in the large slit-pupiled eyes. There was not even any clothing or jewelry that might have helped in telling them apart. Skynx were just skynx.

But Loma seemed to have no trouble recognizing the skynx that came surging into her room on rapid steps of its paddles. "Good Tollsday, Seephaa," she said, bobbing her head.

The skynx raised the front half of its body, elevating its broad arrow-shaped head. "Good Tollsday," said Seephaa in the same piping sing-song voice of every other skynx. "To you and to your..." it paused a long moment, tilting its head as the big eyes looked at Denny. "Friend."

"His name is Denning Carrelson," Loma said.

"Denning Carrelson." The skynx pronounced the name carefully. The big eyes studied Denny again. "I have seen you. You are the one who dances."

Denny nodded. "That's me," he said. He thought about doing a little dance step, but somehow, it felt wrong. Foolish. "You've seen me at the spaceport?"

"That is where I've see you," the skynx agreed. A thin, translucent pink tongue slid from the skynx' mouth and moved quickly across its scarlet lips before sliding back. "And now I see you are here."

"He is just visiting me," said Loma.

The skynx' head bobbed up and down. The eyes turned toward the old woman. "Yes, I see that. However, he has not visited you before."

Denny was surprised to see a flicker of what might have been fear slip across Loma's face. He had always thought that maybe she lived here among the skynx because she liked them better than humans, but watching her talk to this skynx, this Seephaa, it seemed that things between them were not like Denny would have expected. They did not seem to be friends.

Loma's expression hardened. "Denny has come to tell me something."

"Has he?"

"Yah." She looked into the big eyes of the skynx and nodded. "He's come to tell me all humans are to be consigned soon."

The raised head tilted a bit back and forth, the focus of the eyes slipping from Loma to Denny and back again. "And now that he has told you," said Seephaa, "I'm sure that he would like to return to the human area."

Denny started to say that he would like to stay longer. There were things he still wanted to ask Loma, but before he could do more than open his mouth, the skynx dropped to the floor, turned, and moved smoothly back through the curtain.

Loma looked at the still swaying curtain. "Whatever you're going to do," she said, "do it soon."

I 2

The skynx sent Denny home in a road ferry. It looked just like one of the ones the cithians used on the outside, but inside it was divided into many little couches, Overhead, a little nozzle sprayed a fine mist, making the whole inside of the ferry damp, and the windows were heavily shaded, keeping everything dim. Denny had never been inside one of the ferries that the cithians used, but he didn't think they would find this one very comfortable.

For the first few minutes of the ride, Denny had been busy looking at the way water trickled through the inside of the ferry, and at the way other ferries moved around it on the road. He had ridden on the ground transports many times, and they moved faster than the ferries, but a ground transport had a tunnel or a rail all to itself, and just the way the ferry had to move around made the ride seem more exciting. Many times it seemed that they were going to collide with another ferry, and more than once it seemed to Denny they were about to run down a molting cithian trying to cross the street on clumsy, soft legs, but the ferry moved on around each obstacle.

There was only one skynx in the ferry with Denny, and as far as Denny could tell, the skynx was doing nothing to steer the vehicle's movements. The long body lay sprawled along the length of one of the couches, paddles tucked neatly out of sight. The skynx' eyes were closed. Every now and then, the pink tongue came out to lick at a passing rivulet of water, but otherwise the skynx seemed to be asleep.

After a while, Denny got tired of watching the movements of the ferries and the passing buildings. He got as close to the small window as he could, and opened up his book.

Loma had given him the book as he was leaving. Like with the Count book, Denny had a hard time with it at first. He knew a lot of the words, but he wasn't used to seeing so many words together in the same place. Of course, there were words he didn't know. Words like "forest" and "winter." Words he'd heard in some of the old songs, but never thought to ask about.

The thing that surprised Denny most about the book as he puzzled it out by the blue-white light through the window, was that even though it did have humans in it, the book was about another kind of people, one he'd never heard of. If the book was as old as Loma said, then it must have come from Earth. Denny had never realized there were other people on Earth besides humans. The people in the book, the people called "dogs," seemed like a good sort of people. Brave people.

Denny wondered if any of these dogs had been rescued from poor used-up Earth when the cithians came to save the humans from their awful mistakes. Some of the humans in the story were cruel to the dogs, but not all were. Some of the people and dogs seemed to get along well enough. It would be sad to think they were all gone. Maybe Omi would know.

13

PAIRDAY

On Pairday, Denny became a criminal. In one way, that really didn't seem like much of a change, since the cithians often acted like humans had done something wrong, no matter what they had done. Even though they had been told it was okay to walk around town, cithians were always drumming at Denny, or stopping him, or acting like he was somewhere he shouldn't be. Other humans got treated the same way. Or worse. Even Cousin Kettle, despite his uniform and his job, was always getting thrown off the transport or treated like he'd done something bad. Once the authority had held him for two days, in a tiny room with no lights or windows, and they never even said why.

The difference was that this time Denny really had done something wrong. Or at least, something that he knew cithians would think was wrong.

Early on Pairday, with both suns up and spiraling slowly toward the center of the sky, Denny left his own place and went down the hall to the lift. Cousin Sirah and Cousin Yulia were there, talking quietly. As Denny came closer, Sirah smiled. Yulia had her usual worried look. Then Sirah saw what Denny was carrying, and her smile turned to a frown.

"You're not," she said.

Denny shifted the box in his arms and shrugged. "I guess I am," he said.

Sirah peered over the rim of the box. "But that was one of my favorites."

The lift arrived and Denny stepped on. "They're all my favorites," he said.

Sirah and Yulia rode with him to the ground, and then Denny headed out on the street, back to the block of buildings that had been turned into Poppa Jam's Porium. This time, Jam already had the door open when Denny arrived. Cousin Haw was carrying a big chair toward the back of the store, while Poppa Jam leaned on the counter, waving warm air toward his face with a plastic fan.

Poppa Jam looked up, saw Denny, looked away, then looked back at him again. The old man's wooly eyebrows shot up. "Well now," he said. "Look at this." He put his palms flat on the counter top and straightened himself. "Come on in."

Denny hesitated a step, then came over to the counter and sat down his tattered box. "I'm interested in selling this," he said.

Poppa Jam pushed Denny's hands away and tugged at the pressed paper side of the box. The box tore open under Poppa Jam's eager attention. Inside was a piece of metalwork not more than two or three hands high. A piece of what Denny's father had called "sculpture."

It wasn't possible to say exactly what it was. On the other hand, it was also hard to say exactly what it *wasn't*. The whole thing had been made from bits and strips of different metals that Denny's father had worked with hammer and heat into a swirl of shapes, colors, and textures. Looked at one way, it seemed like the base of the thing was a dark iron sea, where something sleek was forcing its way up from tumbling waves. Seen another way it looked like a hand pressing down, weighted by links of bronze and green-stained copper. Were these little rust-flecked bits the shapes of small creatures trying to escape the teeth of something larger? Was the jagged edge a line of figures ascending a long stair? No...but also yes.

Poppa Jam let out a long sigh—the kind of sound someone might make when they ate something really nice. "Now this is worth some picture books," he said.

"I don't want picture books," said Denny.

"You don't?" Poppa Jam's eyes came up to meet Denny's. "What is it you want?"

"I need a maton."

Denny had never seen the color leave someone's face as fast as it did Jam's. "You..." Jam stopped, looked around the Porium, then continued in a whisper. "You know better. Humans aren't allowed to have those things."

"I know we're not allowed. But do you have one?"

"No." Sweat appeared on Poppa Jam's forehead. "I don't have one. Never had one. Of course I don't have one. Don't know why anyone would want one." He looked back into the store. "Now, I have some things here you'd like. I've got..."

"If you don't have a maton," said Denny. "Then where can I get one?"

Poppa Jam ran a hand across his sweaty face and gave a nervous laugh. "You can't. You don't get one. Humans aren't allowed to have them."

"Oh. Okay." Denny dragged the torn box toward him and carefully got his arms under the little metal sculpture. "I guess I'll take this back."

Poppa Jam reached a hand across the counter. "Wait," he said. "I'll make a deal with you." He wiped at his face again with his free hand. "The klickiks, they really like these things. You let me sell this one to them, and I'll give you..." He paused a moment and Denny saw Jam's eyes go up and to the side as he thought the deal through. "Half," he said at last. "I'll give you half the credits."

"Do they have a maton?"

"No!" Poppa Jam's voice soared past whisper and right into a shout. "Earth, boy, will you stop asking about that? The klickiks will give you good credits. Red credits. Maybe even blue."

Denny tugged the box free and stepped back from the counter. "I don't need any credits."

"Everyone needs credits." Poppa Jam started around the end of the counter. "With credits, you can get whatever you want. Whatever..."

"Can I get a maton?"

"No, but you can get..."

"Whatever they'll let us have," said Denny.

Cousin Haw came out of the shelves, gnawing at a block of orange chez. "What's going on?"

"Nothing," said Denny. He shifted the broken box and started toward the open front of the Porium. "I was just leaving."

Every now and then Auntie Talla managed to lay hold of enough sugar to make backla or just-pie. When Denny was little, he looked forward to those times more than anything else in the worlds. He remembered a day when his father had been slow to start out for Restaurant, and Denny had practically jumped out of his skin worrying that they would be too late to get their small, sweet share. As Denny started out the door, that same feeling seemed to come over Poppa Jam.

The old man came around the counter actually wringing his hands. "Think now, There's got to be something that you want."

"There is," Denny said, still half turned toward the door.

Poppa Jam winced. "Don't say..."

"I need a maton."

"What's a maton?" Haw said, rather loudly, from halfway across the store.

This time Poppa Jam didn't just wince, he looked like someone had punched him in the stomach. "Shut it, Haw," he said. He looked at Denny and drew a deep breath. "Look, kid, you want the picture book? It's a deal. You want pops? Take a dozen. But I can't trade you a maton, because I don't have a maton."

Denny thought for a moment, "If these dasiks like my dad's stuff so much, how do you know they won't trade you a maton for it?"

Poppa Jam shook his head, "No. They won't. You have to trust me. Trading with all these guys is what I do, and I can tell you none of them is going to give a human any kind of complex electronics, like a maton. It's against the rules. The big rules."

"But...why?" asked Denny.

"Does it matter?" Poppa Jam said with a shrug.

Denny opened his mouth to say more, but really, there was no more to say. Instead, he turned slowly and left the Porium. Behind him, he could hear Poppa Jam saying something to Cousin Haw. He sounded angry.

Without a maton, there was no way to tell what else was on the memory the chug had given Denny. Maybe it didn't matter. After all, the only thing they'd been able to see with Loma's reader was the story about the old disease, and Denny couldn't see how that mattered to anyone. It was just a story from old Earth. A dead story, like the ones in Loma's books. Probably the whole thing was just trash, something the chug was throwing away.

Denny was almost back to the compartment house when someone came hurrying up beside him. He was surprised to see that it was Cousin Yulia, hunched in her big coat. Fear, yes, but it wasn't just fear.

"Did you find something at the Porium?" Denny asked.

"Yes," said Yulia, then, "No. I mean...nothing I have the credits to buy." She glanced over at Denny, looked away, then glanced at him again. She bit her lip so hard Denny could see the lip turn white.

"What's wrong?" he asked. "Do you want to borrow some credits?"

"It's not that. It's...I know."

"Know what?"

Cousin Yulia moved around to step in front of Denny. "I know where you can find a maton."

14

Yulia looked quickly around the street. Then she surprised Denny by reaching over and grabbing at his hand. "Come this way," she said.

Denny opened his mouth to reply, but before he could get a word out he found himself stumbling forward as Yulia tugged him quickly across the cracked street toward the long-abandoned building that stood opposite the Porium. Only when they were in the deep shadows beyond the sagging blue doors did she finally release him.

"What are you talking about?" Denny asked. "How can you know about matons?"

Yulia's pale eyes flicked left and right and Denny could see her throat work as she swallowed hard. "I was in the Porium. I heard what you were saying. I..." She peeked out at the street and quickly took a step back into the shadows. "Come over here." She stepped away from him, nearly disappearing along the dim hallway.

Denny hesitated for a moment, and then followed her into the gloom. He had never liked this building. It wasn't very tall, just a half dozen floors, but the upper levels leaned in on themselves like carelessly stacked plates. Years of being open to the weather – and years of humans carrying off parts of the building for other uses – had left the place with warped walls, leaky ceilings, and floors with cracked and missing tiles. The lift had long ago stopped running, and the pipes and wires had long been hauled away. Down on the bottom floor there were chairs, lots of chairs, but they were far too small for most humans and not even Poppa Jam could be bothered to cross the street to collect them. Denny had sometimes wondered if the building had once been used by some other kind of people. Someone like humans, only smaller.

On top of everything else, the place smelled bad. Stale and moldy. As Denny tried to keep up with Yulia, he could hear the soft movement of little creatures around him. Scuttles, certainly. Maybe scats. Denny's father had always told him to stay out of this place. It was one rule that Denny had never really been tempted to break.

Yulia went down the hall, stepping around a jumbled pile of the undersized chairs and past a long row of tall metal boxes that were lined against one wall. The doors of the boxes hung open, and there was just enough light for Denny to see peeling flakes of green paint separated by wide patches of rust. Inside the boxes there was nothing but darkness. He tried to imagine what had once been kept in this place, but it was just another thing that had long been forgotten.

Yulia's footsteps made a soft crunching as she walked across clumps of fallen plaster and stepped into a room at the end of the hall. She disappeared into shadows. Denny came forward slowly, waving his hand to feel ahead. He felt nothing. Saw nothing. The darkness was absolute.

"Yulia?"

There was a popping sound ahead, and suddenly there was light. Denny blinked. Not light, but lights, a whole series of tiny, bright, blue-white lights appeared overhead. At first they seemed like just a mess, but as Denny took another step, it seemed to him that there was something half familiar about these little glimmering points.

Under the faint glow, Denny could see that most of the room around him had been cleared away. There was rubble in the corners, along with still more of the too-small chairs, but the center of the room was empty, and more or less clean. On the walls there were old pieces of paper, stained brown by time and curled at the edges. Some of the paper had splotches of faded colors. One of them looked at first like it had words, but after a moment Denny realized it was just all the letters shoved next to each other.

He looked up again at the lights. They were clearly not part of the old structure. Thin wires had been stuck to the moldy ceiling with lots of tacks and handfuls of gloop. From the wires, hair-thin lines descended, each one tipped in light. "Who did this?"

Yulia shrugged, her shoulders moving up and down beneath her oversized jacket. "I did." She stepped to the center of the room and sat down in the clean space, crossing her legs as she settled onto the hard floor.

Denny took a step closer. Some of the lights dangled down far enough that they floated in front of his eyes. Others seemed to be fixed hard against the stained plaster. Again he had the feeling that there was something to them. Something he should know.

"I thought there was no power over here," said Denny.

"There's power," Yulia replied. She shifted around a little, pulling her feet up under her legs. "You just need to know how to find it, and how to hook it up."

Denny stared down at her for a moment, then picked a spot a pace or two away and joined her on the floor. The concrete felt cold through his thin clothing. "But why?"

She shrugged again. "I wanted a place of my own. Not like the compartment. More like...like where I used to be when I was still with my parents."

It took Denny a moment to remember. "You came from Halitt Plex, right? Did they have lights like these?"

"Sort of," said Yulia. "They had stars."

Stars. Denny glanced up again at the sprawl of tiny lights. Sometimes, only in the darkest part of Dimday, and only if you were in just the right place, you could see the stars. They were faint—so faint that you couldn't look at them straight on. You had to see them from the corner of your eye. And even then it was just one or two stars, or maybe a handful if you were lucky. There were nowhere near as many stars as there were lights on Yulia's ceiling.

Denny started to say something, but Yulia tipped her head back, her thick curls falling from her face as the bluish lights reflected in her eyes. "Halitt Plex wasn't like here. For one thing, it was colder. My father said it was north, but I don't really know what that means."

North. Denny rolled the word around in his mind. He had heard it before. No. He had seen it. He'd seen it in Loma's book. "Was it cold there?"

Yulia nodded. "Colder than here, anyway. There wasn't just a little frost on Dimsday. Sometimes there was real snow."

Snow was another word that Denny knew from the book Loma had given him. He thought that maybe he should tell Yulia about the book with the dog people, but first..."You said you know where to get a maton."

She hesitated, and then nodded. The green light shining down left shadows across her cheeks and around her eyes. "Like I said, Halitt Plex was different. It was a lot smaller. It was a new city, not like Jukal. There were no big sleeping stadiums. No real units at all. And no human quarter."

"No quarter?" Denny sat down across from her. The floor was cold through the thin fabric of his pants. "Where did you live?"

"With the cithians."

Denny would have been less surprised if Yulia had told him she had lived on the blue sun. "They let you stay with them?"

"Well, not exactly." Yulia rocked back, looking off into the shadowy corners of the room.

15

YULIA'S STORY

Hallitt Plex was the end of the world. Or at least, the end of the land.

There were no real oceans on Rask, but there were many large lakes and swamps and marshes that stretched on to the horizon in every direction. Hallitt was perched on a long sliver of low ground, flanked on one side by dull gray water and on the other side by dull gray swamp. It was bitter cold on Dimsday, barely above freezing on Whetsday, and raked by sharp winds on every day. It was one of the few places on crowded old Rask that cithians had never lived. For good reason.

But then a survey team found minerals beneath the little swamp island, minerals that were valuable across the planet and off the planet. So cithians came to build a new settlement at Hallitt, and they brought humans with them.

At first there were so few cithians in Hallitt that it was more an outpost than a village. When Yulia was born, there were actually more humans in Hallitt than there were cithians. Humans were everywhere. Humans worked in the mines. Humans drained away the swamps and built long dikes that made the island bigger. Humans built the new city where everyone would live.

Of course, humans didn't do this by themselves. Humans didn't have the skills or knowledge to build the mines, or plan the dikes or design the buildings. Cithians did all that. Humans just did the work.

All the humans in Hallitt Plex had jobs. Even Yulia was given a job when she was still very small. There had been a big, flat belt that came out of the mine carrying rocks to a building where they were crushed. Some of the rocks were the right kind of rocks, the valuable kind. These were blue. Some of the rocks were not the right kind. They were brown or black or gray or sometimes blue—only the wrong kind of blue. It was Yulia's job to reach onto the moving belt, pull off the rocks that were the wrong kind, and throw them onto a pile. There were other children, and sometimes old people, who also did this job. They would stand in a line, grabbing out the not-right rocks, and tossing them away. Every day Yulia's hands were wet and cold and bruised from the rocks, but she did a good job. She worked hard.

Other people had the job of coming for the not-right rocks with little carts and carrying them to the edge of the island, where these rocks were used in making the dikes. They were not right for making whatever it was that was made from the blue rocks, but they were fine for making the low walls that kept out the water. Nothing went to waste in Hallitt.

There were many other sorts of jobs. Few of the cithian crops would grow at Hallitt, so Yulia's mother worked in a building where bright yellow cathik and bright green wheat were grown under banks of lights. Yulia's mother, whose name was Nata, tended the plants, and cut the plants, and ground the plants to flour. Nata's job was also very hard. She came home at the end of each long shift aching from the work she had done all day, but sometimes she was allowed to bring some of the flour home with her. When she did, she and Yulia would use it right away to make flat bread. Which was somehow better than any other flat bread Yulia had ever eaten, even the flat bread made by Auntie Talla, which was very good.

Yulia's father had a different sort of job. He worked in building the city, but he didn't work with a hammer or push a cart like most of the humans. Yulia's father went every day to the place where the new city was being built. He helped the cithians in putting in pipes and in putting in wires. He knew a lot about how the city was to be built. Even the cithians said he was very smart—for a human.

On Dimsday, when the cithians slept, the humans would keep working. On those days, the cithians would sometimes tell Yulia's father what to do, and he would tell the other humans. Her father's name was Bram, but people called him Uncle Boss. Sometimes, after Yulia had worked most of the day, her father would take her to see the new city being built. He showed her how the wires brought power through the city and how the pipes brought water. He showed her how to connect the wires, and how the water was controlled by valves. He showed her how stone and sand and water could go together to make concrete, which could make walls that would not only go up and down, but could also make curves and arches and domes. He showed Yulia how some of the buildings in the new city would be one shape, and some would be another. Together all the different shapes would form a unit, where all the buildings went together to provide supplies and workshops and places to sleep and places to do other things. Hallitt would have two of these units, and when they were done it would be Hallitt Plex—Hallitt the city—and they would all have big warm buildings with lots of space.

At the very end of Dimsday, when the sky was, Bram would take Yulia through the growing city to its south edge, where both of them would stand on one of the new dikes and look out across the swamp to where lights glowed on the horizon. The lights were from the crew laying tracks for the new ground train that would link

Hallitt to other cities. Every Dimsday the tracks were closer. Every Dimsday the buildings were higher. Every Dimsday the stars were bright overhead.

Bram was very excited about living in the new city. Yulia was excited too. Where they lived was not big and certainly not warm. The cithians had long, curved-top buildings where they worked, slept, and did their planning. The humans lived under their cithians, in rooms carved out of the frozen ground that never melted. Yulia and her mother and her father lived with two other families beneath one of the cithian buildings, in a space so low she couldn't stand up, even as a child. Because the cithians liked Yulia's father, they had extra room. But not much. For sleeping they all huddled together, wrapped in many, many blankets. Even then the cold would soak in and in and in until by the time she woke Yulia's hands and feet would ache, then burn, then ache some more.

One Dimsday, when Yulia was twelve, her father came to the mine to find her. By then, Yulia didn't work on the belt as a picker anymore. That was a job for small children. Instead she walked in and out of the mine, following the moving belt, making sure that no rocks got stuck inside all the rollers that made it go. Being a belt walker was an important job. If the belt got stuck, the mine would have to stop until it was fixed. Yulia's mother and Yulia's father were both proud that Yulia had been trusted to do such an important thing, even though working inside the mine could be dangerous.

That Dimsday, Bram was even more excited than usual. The train had reached Hallitt a few days before, and now train after train was coming, bringing all the supplies that a city needed. All the buildings were almost finished. It was almost time for everyone to move to the new buildings. Yulia's father could barely wait to show it all to her. Yulia said that she could not come. She was too dirty from working all day at the mine.

Her father said that was nonsense. Even though it was Dimsday, and very cold, he took off his own coat and wrapped it around Yulia to hide her tattered jacket. Then he walked on in his shirtsleeves, saying that he was not cold at all.

There were many more cithians around than there had been before. Yulia thought many of the cithians seemed upset that a human was going in and out of their buildings. Some of them even rose up on their back legs and sounded their clackers in protest. Yulia's father said she should not be afraid. "They're new here," he said. "They don't know how we do things in Hallitt Plex." He said the "Plex" part with a big smile. After so long on the edge of things, now they were a real city.

Her father took Yulia first to see the new sleeping stadium, which was the biggest building she had ever seen. There were ranks and ranks of sleeping cradles arranged in big circles for the cithians. Even though there were no cithians inside the building yet, it was already deliciously warm. Yulia asked where the humans would sleep.

"I don't know," said her father, tousling Yulia's curly hair. "Maybe this time they will give us the top level."

He took her next into the big square workshops, then into some of the smaller control rooms, and then through one of the stations for the ground train. It was all new. All amazing. Yulia's father could not help showing her things about how the buildings were designed. He was proud of how his work, and the work of many other humans, had helped build the Plex.

Finally he took Yulia into one of the huge domes at the center of each unit. The domes were full of shelves and the shelves were full of...everything. Crates and boxes and barrels. Casks and packages and cans. Not every shelf was full, but the trains had been coming and coming and coming with new things ever since the tracks reached Hallitt.

For the first time in her life, Yulia saw dasiks. She had been told there were other kind of people than cithians and humans, but Hallitt was too cold for most of them. Now that the new buildings had come, dasiks had come with them. Long lines of dasiks were carrying things in from the trains and putting them on the shelves. To Yulia the dasiks looked very big, and their teeth seemed very sharp. Her father only laughed.

"They work with the cithians," he said. "Just like us. We all work together."

Bram took Yulia into one of the aisles that ran between the high shelves. The variety of sizes and shapes that rose up around her made Yulia a little dizzy. "What are all these things?" she asked. And he told her.

Later, they stood on the south wall, the way they had on many other Dimsdays, and looked out over the frozen land. The tracks were finished. The city was finished. Everything looked very different than it had the first time Yulia could remember coming to that place. Only the stars overhead seemed the same.

While they were walking back to their home, two cithians stopped them. These were not strangers. They were cithians that had worked with Yulia's father for years while the city was being built, only this time there were several dasiks with them. The cithians asked Bram to come with them, and he agreed.

"I will see you at home," Yulia's father told her. "Tell your mother to pack up our things. It's time to move."

Yulia might have said that they had very little to pack; just a few cooking things and a few worn clothes and a few old blankets. The blankets were all stiff and smelly and impossible to keep clean. All the way home, Yulia thought how nice it would be to leave the old blankets behind and sleep in the warm sleeping stadium instead. When she got home, her mother was not there. She waited. But it was cithians who came, cithians and dasiks. Yulia was put on a train the next day. She never saw either of her parents again.

16

When she was done with her story, Yulia stood up. "It's very warm in Jukal," she said, as she shifted inside her oversized coat. "But somehow I'm always cold." She walked out, brushing aside stars as she went.

Denny stayed there for a long time, under Yulia's stars. Finally, when he thought he understood what he needed to do, he stood and walked out of the dark room. It was almost surprising to find that it was not Dimsday outside, the way it had been in Yulia's story, but still the same Pairday it had been when Denny had followed her across the street. He didn't see Yulia anywhere as he crossed back over the cracked pavement.

When Denny came back into the Porium, Poppa Jam looked at him with cautious hope. "Decide there was something else you needed after all?"

Denny sat the torn box back onto the counter, and nodded. "Yes." He thought for a moment and pointed across the counter. "I still want the picture book," he said. Then he turned and nodded toward the rear of the store. "And I want some other stuff."

17

DIMSDAY

It took Denny two trips to bring his purchases and other supplies to the old building at the edge of the human quarter. He had no way to lock the doors, and no way to explain what he was doing to anyone who saw him carrying his burden to the building. Denny wasn't sure that anyone had ever said they weren't allowed in the unused authority buildings, but he was pretty sure no one had ever said that they were. If one of the cithians stopped him, Denny would probably be in serious trouble. No chez for three days sort of trouble. Maybe worse. But he saw no one.

There were only two rooms inside the old building. The first one was cleaner, with a series of benches, but it also had a window that looked back into the quarter, a window someone might look through. Denny dragged all his things into a corner of the second room. This room had no windows. One wall of the room was lined with water pipes and nozzles. There was a dented metal sheet at one end, which would come in handy. The room smelled bad, an ugly mix of rotting wood and chemicals. When Denny came in, there were red scuttles as big as Denny's hand gnawing at some paperboard boxes. The scuttles moved out of his way slowly, like they were irritated about being disturbed. There were some chairs at the side of the room, but the scuttles had also gnawed at them, grinding them down until they were barely more than the ghosts of chairs. They surely weren't sturdy enough to sit on. Denny wrinkled his nose and put this things on top of a sagging box.

Carefully, he pulled out the spare clothing he'd brought in his duffle and began to assemble his disguise. There was a thick sweater that had belonged to his father. Two shirts, three belts, two pairs of pants, and a bag full of towels and rags. Denny meant to wear it all.

He put the extra set of pants in front of him, and looped a couple of belts together to hold them in place. Then he stuffed rags down the legs. He put an extra shirt on over his shirt, and stuffed more clothes into the arms. When all the human clothes were on, Denny took the bolts of the thick, coarse cithian cloth that had come from Poppa Jam's Porium, and began wrapping it around himself.

It took longer than Denny had hoped to finish winding the cloth around his face and body. By the time he stumbled toward the stained square of metal to see how he looked, Denny was sweating and feeling very uncomfortable under the many layers of cloth. The clothing, which included an old coat that Denny had outgrown and the blanket from his father's unused bed, bulked Denny up until his figure seemed nearly round as a ball. He had taken special care to wrap up his shoulders so that his head and body seemed all of a piece, with little sign of a neck, and his hands were reduced to vague mitteny shapes. But the strangest thing was that the figure in the glass had both an extra set of arms and a spare set of legs.

Denny shoved a pair of socks onto the end of the extra legs. Some mittens he had never used onto the arms. The extra set of arms was positioned below his own, where the mid-limbs would be on a cithian. Denny tried raising and lowering his real arms, and saw that the fake set moved with him—though not very much. For the fake legs, he'd put the cloth-filled pants actually in front of his own so that with every step the extra limbs would bounce along. He could move, but he sure wasn't going to do any dancing.

He reached down clumsily, barely able to bend inside all the layers, picked up the biggest thing he had purchased from Poppa Jam, and hung it on his back. The plastic moltling shell wasn't heavy, but it took Denny a few tries to get the straps tied while reaching backwards with his wrapped up arms. When he finally got it in place and turned around again, his reflection showed a cithian moltling.

Denny stared through a slit in the cloth bindings. The figure in the glass looked a little lumpy, a little uneven, but so did a lot of moltlings. He crouched forward, and then took a slow step, letting his body tilt to the side. Then he took another slow step with the other leg. The motion didn't look right at first, but Denny backed away and approached the glass again, this time taking care to bend his knees less, extend his legs further. He pulled his hands up, holding them at the level of his shoulders, letting the extra set of arms bob a bit at each step. Then he backed away and did it again.

When he thought his movements looked enough like Omi's, and those of the other moltlings Denny had seen in the street, Denny picked up the eyepad shield that was the last of the items he had gotten from the Porium, and slid it onto his face. The tint of the shield was so dark that Denny had trouble seeing anything at all, but he hoped the heavy glass would keep anyone from noticing his very human eyes peering through a slit in the cloth wrapping.

He wished he had time to practice more, but he worried that if he stayed too long in the old building, he would be caught. After all, the building where the few remaining guards rested was right across the street. Denny shuffled to the door, sending more of the scuttles running as he crossed the room. He twisted around to get the plastic shell through the opening, and stepped outside.

There was no one in the narrow street near the old gate to the quarter. Denny moved as quickly as he could to reach the next corner, then settled into the slow, tilting shuffle that he hoped looked like that of a moltling. Already he was sweating under the many layers of cloth. The plastic shell, which had felt not so very heavy at first, swayed against his back and the straps dug into his shoulders at each step. Though the dark eyepad shield he could see only a vague outline of the street ahead. It was like walking in the darkest part of Dimsday, with no lights anywhere. He kept walking, concentrating on making the right turns to get to his destination.

Denny had always been kind of happy that there wasn't a big cithian work complex very close to the human quarter, because it let him walk around without running into too much trouble, but now he sort of regretted it. Because he needed a work complex to find what he needed, which meant that he had a long walk ahead in his uncomfortable disguise. He sweated his way past one big block of smaller buildings after another. It was the same curving road he had followed on his long walk to see Loma, only this time Denny found every step to be an effort. After a few minutes, he found he didn't have to fake the wobbly side to side walk of a moltling, because he really was that close to tipping over.

He had been walking for close to an hour before he reached a place where there were road ferries regularly moving along the street. He stayed far over to the side, as he had seen real moltlings do, and kept traveling at his slow pace. At first, he was sure that every ferry was about to stop, and that the cithians were sure to see through his disguise, but they just kept moving. Denny even passed a moltling moving in the other direction. Like Omi, this moltling was nearing the end of its soft period. It had discarded most of the cloth wrapping, and its feet were hard enough to clack against the pavement. Denny held his breath as it drew near, but the young cithian passed him quickly, never even turning its eyepads his way.

Finally, when he'd walked so far that his wrappings were damp with sweat, Denny came to one of the circular complexes with a dome-shaped building at its center and a series of taller blocky buildings around it. Following Cousin Yulia's instructions, he turned into one of the narrow paths that angled in toward the central dome. A trio of adult cithians went past, close enough that Denny might have reached out and touched the nearest, but none of them turned or showed any sign of seeing the human behind the cloth and plastic. Denny had the sudden urge to go back. Better yet, to tear off the layers of clothing, discard all the rags, throw the stupid shell on the ground and just run back to the quarter. But he didn't. Keeping himself to the slow tilt-step-tilt shuffle of a moltling, he went into the opening of the dome.

There was no door or curtain that Denny could see, but between one awkward step and the next the air became much cooler. There was a dry, sort of metallic smell and the distant sound of voices, but at first Denny didn't see any cithians at all. What he saw looked kind of like Poppa Jam's Porium...but only if the Porium had been much, much larger. Ahead of him, the building was filled with rings of shelves. These were stocked with boxes of every size, most of them in shades of yellow or brown or red. The shelves were at least twice as tall as Denny. Cutting through this series of rings were aisles that shot straight toward the center, where a tall round tower rose up out of sight toward the top of the dome. Somewhere overhead a a ring of white globes glowed, but the light barely cut through the gloom of the huge space.

Denny stood there, the sweat cooling against his skin, and wondered what to do next. Cousin Yulia had told him that the cithians kept everything in buildings like this, making them available to the zone of buildings that surrounded each storage dome. In Halitt Plex, her father had been one of several humans who actually worked for the cithians, helping to create a new section. The humans thought that they would be living in the section with the cithians, and that one of the buildings near the dome was for them. Only when the section was finished, the humans began to be consigned. Cousin Yulia ended up in Jukal Plex. Her father didn't. She'd never seen any of the other humans she'd known from before.

But just knowing that the cithians kept everything in a storage dome didn't help as much as Denny had thought it would. Because the cithians kept everything in the storage dome. Everything. The dome was huge. There was also another problem, because now that he really thought about it, Denny had no idea what a maton looked like.

He scanned the row of boxes in the nearest shelf. He didn't know if he should be looking at those as small as his hand, or those large enough to hide a whole cithian. He took a clumsy step forward.

"Objective," said a voice.

Denny jumped, which made the plastic shell rise and thump against his back. He twisted around awkwardly, trying to see who was speaking, but there was no one near.

"Objective," said the voice again.

As far as Denny could tell, the voice was coming from nowhere. Or maybe everywhere. "Hello?"

"Objective."

"Uhh..." He thought about making something up. After all, if there was a cithian watching him from somewhere else in the big room, the cithian might have already noticed that Denny didn't look quite right, or didn't sound like a moltling. There could already be cithians from the authority on the way, or a team of dasik guards ready to hurry Denny to consignment. Only Denny didn't see anyone. Plus, there was something about the voice. It was sort of not real, like the voice that came from the buttons on the dasik uniforms.

"I need a maton," he said.

"Specify model," said the voice.

"Uhh..." Denny said again. He wasn't sure what the voice meant by "model." He hoped it meant that the voice understood what he was looking for, but he didn't know what to say next. "Do you have a maton?"

"Specify model."

"Can I have one?"

"Specify model."

"Can you show me how to find it?"

"Transaction ended," said the voice. Then after a short pause. "Objective?"

Denny took a deep breath and tried again. "I need a maton."

"Specify model."

"What is a model?"

For a moment, there was no response. Then the voice spoke again. "The following models are available at this facility. Ocelli A. Ocelli A four. Malpighian fourteen. Trochanter B. Trochanter C. Subesophageal Nine..."

"Ocelli," said Denny. "An Ocelli A four. Yes, I want a Ocellia A four model of maton." He had picked it mostly because, of all the models that the voice had listed, this was the easiest to say.

There was no immediate response, and Denny wondered if he had ruined things by interrupting the voice. Then a thin line of yellow-orange appeared on the floor. The line pulsed slightly with light. It led from Denny's feet–his fake, front feet–down the nearest aisle toward the center of the room.

"Thank you," said Denny. The voice did not reply.

Denny began walking across the room. Once away from the door, it was dark enough that Denny had to hold the eyepad shields up with one hand and peek under them to see the line. He forgot, for the first few steps, to keep up his imitation of a moltling's walk. Then he slowed down, hunched over, and started his tilting back and forth. Just because the voice came from something like a maton, didn't mean that there wasn't someone out there watching.

The yellow line carried on past a dozen or more ranks of high shelves, then turned right between two curving rows. Between the shelves Denny felt a bit trapped. The space was narrow enough that the plastic shell tapped against shelves on either side with each rolling step. The top shelf was high above his head, and the curve of the row meant that he could only see a few steps in either direction. He passed by one of the aisles pointing to the tower at the center of the room, but the yellow line kept pointing around the curve, so Denny kept following.

He felt like he had gone so far that he was about to be back where he started, when suddenly the line ended. Denny looked up at the shelves on either side and saw that there were many, many, many boxes, all of them about the size of his head, and none of them with any clear label.

Denny looked up at the shadows overhead. "Where is it?" he said. "Hello?" The voice either couldn't hear him, or wasn't interested.

He took the eyepad shield completely off and set it down on the shelf so he could take a closer look at the boxes around him. If there was any writing on them, or anything at all to tell you what was supposed to be in inside, he couldn't see it. Maybe the cithians could tell what was what by smelling the boxes. Or by tasting them with the little sensors he knew they had on their forelimbs. Denny couldn't do that.

He turned to the shelf on the left and grabbed the box at eye level. Denny thought about turning and leaving, but he also thought how bad it would be to get back to the quarter and discover that what he'd picked up wasn't a maton after all. He fumbled at the box with his cloth wrapped hands. There were some grooves in the package, but they seemed to be designed for the tiny manipulators at the end of a cithian mid-limb, and were way too narrow for Denny to get his fingers in, even when he slipped them out through a gap in the heavy cloth wrapping. He tried to pull the top off, but it wouldn't come. He pressed and poked at the edges, but nothing happened. Finally he simply turned the box over and shook it.

The top came off, and something small, rounded, and silvery fell from the box. Denny dropped the box and tried to catch the object, but it struck the hard floor with a metallic clang and bounced away. Clumsy in his moltling disguise, Denny shuffled after the gleaming ball as it wobbled along between the shelves, but he only managed to kick it with one of his fake front feet, and when he stepped forward to try and catch it, he kicked it harder. The device went spinning away, wobbling and twisting along the aisle. The shape of the device wasn't a perfect sphere, and it tended to roll to one side, but its turn almost exactly matched the curve of the shelves. It just kept rolling and rolling. Denny hurried after it, with his real legs thumping against the empty front legs of his disguise and the spare set of arms bouncing against his chest.

When the silver thing finally fetched up against the bottom of a shelf, Denny bent down to pick it up. The weight of the plastic shell on his back almost caused him to fall over, but with a little arm waving, he managed to stand up again and get his first good look at the device.

There was nothing to it. Just a slightly lumpy silver ball. Denny turned it over carefully, but there were no buttons, no knobs or dials or screens. "Are you a maton?" he said, hoping that the little device might reply. It said nothing.

"Hello?" Still nothing.

Denny looked around. He had walked so far in chasing the fallen device that he couldn't even see the box

it had come from. He went back along the curving aisle...
and stopped.

The fallen box lay in the middle of the aisle. Bending
over it was a cithian. An adult cithian with the red stripe
of the Jukal Plex Legal Authority across its shell.

Denny slowly backed away. When the curve of the
shelf was enough to hide him, he started to walk faster.
When he got to the next aisle that cut across the sets of
shelves, he turned right toward the outside of the
building. Behind him, Denny heard a clicking, scrabbling
sound. A movement sound. He started to run as fast as his
disguise would allow.

He reached the outer wall of the building, but still
couldn't see anything of the door where he had come in.
The wall was a dark gray, and seemed to be nearly
covered in wires, pipes, ducts, and grids, all of them
painted the same color. There were no labels or signs that
Denny could see. Some of the old buildings in the human
quarter had signs above the outside doors that said "Out."
Some of them had arrows on the floor that pointed to
these doors. The cithians apparently didn't believe in
such signs.

Denny wasn't sure which way would take him back to
the door, but he turned right again and kept running. A
few steps later, he skidded to a halt. The bright twin suns
of Pairday were shining right through the broad open
door just ahead, spilling a cone of brilliant light into the
otherwise gloomy space. But silhouetted against that light

was the form of another adult cithian. Denny backed away. He pressed his plastic shell against the wall, peering toward the entrance from around the side of a large pipe.

From out of the shelves, another cithian appeared. It could have been the one Denny saw by the fallen box, but he couldn't really tell. It joined the cithian standing in the entrance. The two cithians bent close together and touched forelimbs, as cithians often did when speaking to each other. After a moment, they moved apart, and both of them headed into the shelves, moving in different directions. Denny gave them ten seconds to get away, then started for the door.

He had barely taken half a step when two more cithians appeared. And two dasiks right behind them. The newcomers didn't hesitate, but started immediately into the stacks, fanning out to cover all the aisles.

"Earth," Denny said, but he said it very, very quietly. He back away until he once again had the shelves sheltering him from the view of the nearest cithian, and then he turned and ran again, staying to the outside. He thought that maybe there was a door on the other side of the tall building, but even if there was, it seemed likely that there would be a cithian or a dasik there, too. In fact, if there was another door, maybe cithians had already come through it. Maybe they were coming toward him. Maybe he was running straight toward them. And what about the cithians who had gone up the center aisles, wouldn't they get to the other side long before Denny made it by going around the outside wall?

He stood against the wall. His breath was coming hard and his heart was beating in his ears. The sweat he had worked up getting to the building was now icy under the many layers of cloth.

One thing was sure, Denny could not get caught. His disguise might fool another cithian if he was just passing them in the street, or even talking to them at a distance, but there was no way the cithians wouldn't notice something strange if they were right beside Denny. For one thing, he didn't even have his eyepad shield. It was still lying on the shelf back where he had been looking for a maton. No cithian was going to look at his eyes peeking out between the folds of cloth and think that he was anything but a human.

Denny imagined the authority cithians grabbing hold of him with the hard manipulators of their forelimbs. He imagined them dragging him through the city. He imagined Overcontroller Hiser looking at him, not in the kindly, protective way that he sometimes did, but in a way that said Denny was in serious trouble. If he was caught now, it wouldn't be just no chez for a week. It meant Hiser telling Denny that he was going to be consigned today, right now, this moment. And not consigned to the place where his father had been sent. Not to a place where anyone had been sent. Consigned to a place where he would never see Cousin Sirah, or

Auntie Talla, or irritating Cousin Kettle, or even Poppa Jam. A place where he might never see another human. Ever.

There was a scraping sound ahead. The sound of a hard cithian foot on a hard floor.

Denny turned left, the plastic shell bumping against the wall made a plonking sound as he moved, which made him wince. He looked left. Right. Then instead of staying near the wall he plunged into the space between the curving shelves. The shelves on one side were all covered with boxes that were bigger than Denny. Here and there, there were gaps in the boxes, and a dozen steps in Denny made a sudden decision. He jumped into one of these gaps, slid between two of the boxes, and lay still.

There was the sound of his breathing, and the pounding of his heart. Otherwise, the whole vast space seemed silent.

It wasn't until he was laying there that Denny realized he was still clutching the silver thing that had fallen from the box in his right hand. He raised it up to his face. His breath misted the silvery sides as he carefully turned if over. It was nothing but a slightly lumpy silver ball. He was going to be sent away for nothing. Only...

Denny brought the thing closer to his face. One spot on its surface was flat. One small, square spot. One spot just about the same size as... He shifted the ball to his left hand, then dug into his pocket and produced the little purple cube the chug had given him.

There was a scrabbling sound nearby. One of the cithians was coming through the space through the shelves right next to Denny. The tap-scrape-tap sound of its long dark, jointed feet on the hard floor came closer, closer... and then it was moving away, walking quickly through the dim space. It had gone past him.

Denny let out a slow breath that until that moment he hadn't realized he had been holding. He raised the silver ball, turned it so that the little square was exposed, then brought the cube up to it. The size was right. Just right. Denny touched the cube to the ball.

His hand exploded in agony.

18

Working...Working...Working...

Memory core...detected.
Neural connection...nonstandard.
Performing transformation matrix.

Tracing...Tracing...Tracing...

Link established.

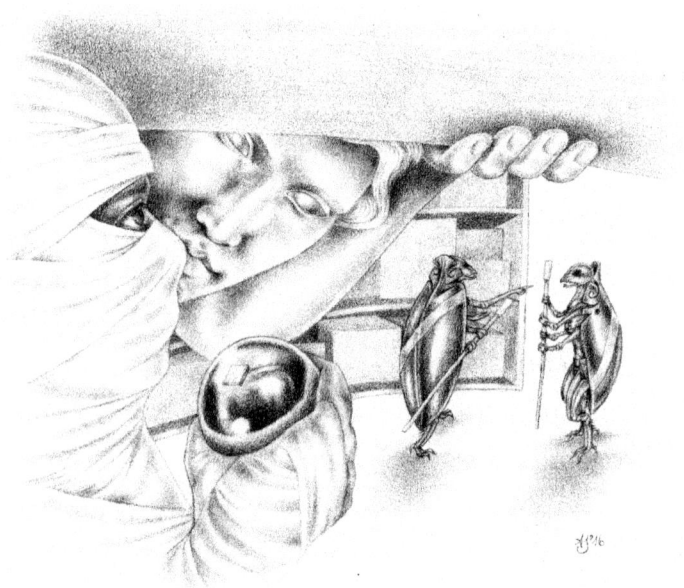

19

The pain was gone. Denny was still lying on the shelf, wedged between two boxes–two kind of blood red boxes, now that he thought about it–bracing himself against the flood of pain. Only there wasn't any pain. Whatever had happened when he touched the cube to the silver ball, it didn't seem like it was happening now.

Denny slowly raised his face to look toward the thing in his hand. He sort of expected to see that his whole hand had been blasted off, but it was still there. So was the maton. He turned it around, noticing that the purple cube seemed to have pulled itself into the silver ball so that it was almost even with the surface. There was just a little rim of purple visible above the silver surface. Except for that, it looked the same.

Just then, he noticed that he wasn't alone. Standing in the space between the shelf where Denny was hiding and the next, was a woman. A human woman.

Denny grunted in surprise, his voice muffled by a layer of cloth that had fallen against his face. He shoved himself back against the boxes. As he bumped against the side of the shelves, the silver ball slipped out of his fingers and rolled away from his hand.

The woman rippled, as if she was painted on a flapping curtain, and vanished.

Denny gulped down a lump in his throat. He twisted around, looking to see where the woman had gone, but there was no one in sight. From somewhere down the next aisle, he heard the sound of a cithian moving quickly past. "Serration 34 unoccupied," said a cithian voice. Another cithian replied. The voice had the weird, muffled sound that came from being on some kind of radio.

The scrabbling sound came again. The cithian was getting closer.

Moving as slowly as he could with his pounding heart and his wrapped-up limbs, Denny slide further back along the shelf, tucking his knees up against his face. The soft form of his fake legs were pressed up against the shelf above him. The plastic shell under his back made him feel unstable, with every breath ready to send him rocking from side to side.

The clack of cithian rear-claws against a hard surface came again. Denny saw the shape of a cithian come around the next line of shelves and start up the row where he was hiding. The cithian had barely taken a step toward him when Denny saw the silver maton. It was lying on the edge of the shelf, tipped so far out into space that it was a wonder that it didn't fall. All the cithian had to do was look down, and he would see the shiny surface of the little orb gleaming in the dim light.

Denny started to reach for it. His fingers were almost on it when he remembered the pain he had felt when touching it the first time. Maybe it was a one-time thing. But then, maybe it wasn't.

The cithian took another slow step. Denny grabbed the sphere.

At once the shock ran through him as if he had swallowed an electric cable. He ground his teeth together to keep from screaming.

The strange woman was back. She was standing right beside the cithian. She was green. Or at least green-ish. Her whole body and face and even what Denny could see of her clothes and hair seemed to be made out of the same thing, some kind of sparkly pale green stone with little flecks of red and white. Denny could see the stony length of her bare legs, and her stone feet laced into stone sandals. He could just see her stone hands dangling below the hem of her stone robe.

The cithian would see her. Had to see her. She was right beside him.

There was a soft beeping sound. "Serration 33 clear," said the cithian, standing no more than an arm's length from Denny. The hard back claws of its rear limbs clattered past as it moved on along the row.

Denny lay very still for several seconds longer. The pain was mostly gone, but his arms and legs still ached, like when he had moved something very heavy or when he ran up the stairs to his compartment on a day when the lift wasn't working. Carefully, making as little noise as possible, Denny leaned to the side to look up at the green woman.

The stone eyes were fixed on his face. There was something funny about the woman's features. She was made out of some kind of rock, which was funny on its own, but it was something more than that. Something about the shape of her nose, the curve of her cheeks, the way her forehead met the rest of her face. She was definitely human–Cousin Sirah had a little of the same look–only she seemed a different kind of human than Denny.

She was absolutely motionless. Frozen. Somewhere, maybe in a picture book, Denny could remember seeing a person carved out of a block of stone. A statue, like the ones his father made of metal, only different. That's what this woman was like. Only not.

Denny glanced at the silvery ball in his hand. He knew that, somehow, it was making this woman. Like the images of the people with the terrible disease that had appeared when the memory had been placed inside Loma's player, this ball was somehow making the image of the woman. She wasn't really there. It was just a picture. Only the picture's that Loma's player made had seemed like just that–pictures floating in the center of the old woman's tiny room. They didn't seem real. But this woman...

The green woman moved. Her arms might look like stone, but they flexed like muscle. The stone robe she was wearing shifted like cloth. There was no center to her red and white flecked eye, but still Denny could tell that she was looking at him.

The stone face leaned in toward him, the stone eyes staring right into Denny's own. "Hello, Denning Carrelson, resident 14723, Human Containment Facility, Jukal Plex, Rask," she said in a bright, friendly, and quite loud tone. "I'm Athena."

It took everything Denny had not to drop the silver ball again. "You know my name," he whispered.

"Oh, yes," said the green woman. She nodded, and the corners of her stony mouth were turned up in a slight smile. "I have access to quite a large store of information."

Denny tried to twist around to see down the row, but with the boxes and shelves all around him and the wrappings, and the extra clothes, and the plastic shell, he could barely see past the woman. "You need to be quiet," he whispered. "They'll hear you."

The woman's smile didn't falter. It almost seemed to Denny like she found the situation he was in funny "Oh no," she said. "I'm speaking to you by direct neural connection. No one else can hear, see, or detect my presence in any way. Which reminds me." The woman straightened herself. "The automation nexus on which this interface is operating is specifically not designed for human operation. Use of this nexus can cause discomfort."

Denny took a second to process her words. "Does that mean every time I touch this ball, it's going to hurt?" The green woman, Athena, nodded. "Also, continued use may lead to medium to long term injury. I am sorry." She was still smiling.

No matter how long he thought about this, it didn't sound good. Denny looked away from the woman at the silver ball as he turned it over and over in his hand. "If I went back to get a different maton..."

"All such devices available in this facility are encoded with similar lock out mechanisms for human use," she said. The woman leaned toward him and winked one stony eye. "They thought it would hurt so much you would never use it. You've surprised them."

"Surprised who?" asked Denny.

Athena raised a hand to her mouth and her eyes widened, then... something happened. Her lips moved, but no sound was produced. Her face and her arm jerked from one position to another in an instant, and she was again looking at Denny with a smile.

He started to ask her again, but just then the sound of cithians moving through the big space returned. From the sound, Denny could tell it was more than one cithian moving his way. At least two. Maybe more. They were coming slowly, and as they approached he heard a slight groan of metal, the sound of something being slid out of the way. The cithians were checking the shelves.

Denny put one hand on the floor and pulled a little more of himself out into the aisle. "Can you help me?" he asked, speaking as quietly as he could.

She knelt down next to him, the edge of her strange stone robe settling over her knees. "I'm sorry," she said, "but my physical interactions are strictly limited." Denny guessed that meant that she couldn't help.

There was most noise from off to Denny's left. More footsteps, and more grating noises of moving boxes. The cithians were no more than two shelves away, and perhaps closer. "Can you tell me how to get out of here?" he asked. "Without being caught?"

Athen's expression remained just the same. "I can direct your actions toward the path most likely to lead to success," she said. She turned her head for a moment, apparently looking toward the tower at the center of the room. "I am interfacing with the automation nexus for this facility."

"Won't they catch you?"

"No," she said simply. After a few seconds, Athena gave an abrupt nod and turned back to Denny. "Come out now," she said.

Denny heaved his way free of the shelves. He could hear the cithians still working their way toward him, and it was difficult to get out without making noise, especially while still holding onto the maton. Athena stood over him as he twisted and wormed his way onto the floor.

"Alacrity is desirable," she said.

"What?"

"Move faster."

Denny made it out from between the shelves and boxes, and struggled to his feet, stepping on one of his own fake feet in the process and almost falling onto his face. Finally he was standing.

"This way," said the green woman. "Follow me."

She headed down the aisle at a fast walk. Denny could hear the slap, slap of her sandals on the floor, but he had to assume that, like her voice, it was a sound made only for him. He was surprised by how tired he felt as he walked after her. The disguise still made him clumsy, but it was more than that. His legs and arms felt weighted down. The plastic shell felt like it was made of thick metal.

"Stop," Athena said suddenly. She raised a hand, and when Denny ran into it he was surprised that he actually felt something, like a slight, but real, pressure against his skin.

From down the aisle, a dark figure moved. A shape flicked toward Denny for a second, then was gone.

"Continue." Athena started moving again, walking even faster than before. Denny struggled to keep up.

He was feeling worse at every step. His head swam. His stomach lurched. "I think I'm going to be sick," he said, speaking louder than he probably should.

Athena turned to look at him with stony smile still in place. "You are feeling the result of prolonged use of the automation nexus. I suggest you stop using the device now to avoid long-term damage."

Denny nodded. He looked at the ball in his hand. His hand was shaking. "How will I talk to you when I put it down?" he asked.

"Communication is impossible without the nexus to mediate," said the green woman. "I'm sorry."

Denny swayed on his feet. If he put the maton down, he wouldn't have Athena to show him out, but if he held on, he might soon be too sick to move. "Get me out of here," he whispered to her. "Quickly."

Athena cut a path across the center of the room. Twice more, she stopped Denny as they waited for cithians to pass, but Denny felt so bad he barely looked up. Finally, they reached the outer wall again. Denny looked around, expecting to see a door nearby, but there were only all the pipes and ducts and wires.

The green woman raised her stone hand to point at a dark gray handle set nearly flush with the dark gray wall. "Pull this down," she said,

Denny stumbled forward. On his first attempt, the cloth-wrapped fingers of his left hand slipped from the handle, but when he tried again it came down. With a slight whoosh of moving air, a small opening appeared on the wall. It was barely as tall as Denny's knees and maybe twice as wide as his shoulders.

"Crawl through there and you'll be outside," said Athena. Her stone eyes studied Denny's face. "Please cease use of the automation nexus immediately to avoid permanent damage."

Denny nodded wearily. His head was splitting, his limbs aching, his stomach rolling over and over. He almost wished the cithians would catch him. Carefully, he tucked his hand into the many folds of cloth over his stomach, then released the maton. At once, he felt a little better. But only a little.

He got down on his knees and looked into the low tunnel. It was short. He would have to take off the plastic shell and drag it behind him, but he could see the bright purplish light of Pairsday shining through the other end of the tunnel.

With a groan, Denny got down on his knees and unstrapped the shell. Moving only a hand at a time, he made his escape through the tunnel. He could feel the compact weight of the maton hidden in the folds of cloth. He hoped it was worth it.

20

WHETSDAY

On Whetsday, Denny learned the truth about the cithians, about the humans, and about his father.

It was only after he had reached the outside of the tunnel that Denny realized that the eyepad shields were still somewhere back inside. Not only that, but the rest of his disguise was tattered and stained. There seemed little chance it would fool a cithian now at any distance.

Denny rolled over, leaning against the outside of the dome-shaped building, and began to unwind the long roll of heavy cloth. It took him a long time to get most of his costume removed, and all the while he expected to see a cithian or dasik come around the building, but finally he stood up and brushed away as much of the dust and grime that was clinging to him as possible. He thought about carrying away his disguise, but a human going through the city with a moltling shell in one hand seemed like a bad idea. Instead he piled all the extra clothing into a heap and placed the shell over it. He shoved the whole mess back into the short tunnel. The dark color of the shell was a good match for the dim light in the tunnel, and it was a long way to either door, so Denny could only hope that it would be some time before someone looked inside. A longer time before someone found the disguise. A really long time before anyone thought that it might have actually been a human inside the building.

With the silver maton carefully wrapped in an old shirt, Denny walked away from the building and angled back to the street. A few cithians saw him as he was rejoining the main road, and one of them drummed out a warning, but Denny didn't think it was anything more than the way he was usually treated as a human out in the city. He lowered his head, gave the cithians plenty of room, and kept walking. Anyway, he still felt all kinds of awful. Like he'd been hit by a road ferry. Or two.

By the time he passed by the old gate and stepped into the human quarter, the blue and red suns had finished their spiraling path through Pairsday and begun moving toward the same point in the bleached white sky. It was Whetsday again.

Denny felt more than a little hungry, but it didn't matter much because he was so thirsty he didn't feel like he could eat. He dragged back down the street to the compartment building, ignoring the glare from Cousin Haw who was standing in the open door of the Porium and exchanging a nod with Auntie Talla who was passing up the street in the other direction in her long going-to-market robe.

The cooling was out in the compartment building–again–but at least the lift was working. Denny leaned against the dented metal wall as the little cube rose upward past all the empty floors to the place where the last humans in the building lived.

He had his thoughts set on getting to his compartment, drinking about a gallon of water, then sleeping until Skimsday, but no sooner had he taken a step down the hall than the door of Cousin Yulia's compartment opened. "Did you get it?" she asked. The thick, loose curls of her hair were bouncing around her head, and for once she looked more excited than afraid.

Denny nodded. He started to say something, but he couldn't get past the dust that was clogging his throat. Then he saw Cousin Sirah coming out of Yulia's compartment to join her in the hallway.

Cousin Yulia turned toward her. "He found one. He has it."

"You have a..." Cousin Sirah glanced at Yulia. "What did you say it was?"

"A maton," said Yulia. "It's a device for accessing... it can do lots of things." She hurried up to Denny, looking him up and down. "Where is it?"

Denny reached into his shirt and pulled out the wrapped ball. Even through the cloth, it felt sort of warm.

Like a sleeping animal. "Here," he said, his voice coming out in a croak.

Yulia leaned over the ball, looking at it with her head tilted to the side. "It's smaller than I thought." She looked up at Denny. "Are you sure it's a maton? Does it work?"

"Yeah." Denny nodded. "Sure."

Cousin Sirah came closer. She glanced at the maton for a second, but quickly turned her attention to Denny. "Are you okay?" She pressed her hand against his forehead. "You don't look good."

Denny cleared his throat, trying to speak more clearly. "I'm fi... fine." He swayed a little on his feet. "Just tired. And thirsty."

Yulia was still staring at the wrapped form of the silver ball. "How does this work?" she asked. "Did you put the memory inside? Does it talk?"

It was Cousin Sirah who answered. "Why don't we let Denny go to his compartment, get some water, take a shower, and change clothes? Then we can all talk."

Yulia frowned, she raised one hand, as if she were going to reach for the maton, but her hand stopped short. "Well..."

Denny nodded in relief. "Thanks," he said, pulling back the maton.

"You look like you need it," said Sirah. She wrinkled her nose. "Besides, you stink." She put her hands on Denny's shoulders and turned him toward his own door. "We'll see you when you're clean."

Denny was too tired to even laugh. He palmed open the door, stumbled into his compartment, and dropped the maton to the floor with a thud.

Several times in the last year, water service to the human quarter had been interrupted. Thankfully, this wasn't one of those days. The water that flowed from the tap was warm, and it had an all too familiar rusty taste. It was absolutely delicious. Denny drank down two big glasses and started on a third before a grumble in his stomach warned him to slow down. Then he stripped the dirty remains of his clothing and literally fell into the douser. He lay there on the floor, letting the hot water pound him, until the ration allowance alarm sounded and the douser slowed to a trickle.

Even then, he had trouble getting on his feet. His right hand, the one that had been holding the maton in the warehouse, ached as if it had been pounded by a hammer, his legs shook. He had clutched the maton several times getting home from the domed building, so he could ask Athena which way to go, or what to do, without drawing the attention of the cithians. Every time there had been that burst of pain, and every time he let go of the maton, he had felt more drained. Denny thought about what the green woman had said, about the possibility of long term damage. He thought maybe he had already touched the thing for too long.

Still, by the time he had climbed out of the douser and gotten into some clothes that had only a few holes in them, Denny felt better. He fished around in the front storage bin, found a half block of chez, and carried it into the front room. He had not stood in the line for food that morning. Or the morning before. The old chez had turned a darker shade of orange, and was a little leathery, but it tasted more or less the same as always.

In the old days, before so many people had been consigned, the cithians might have noticed when a human failed to show up for food two days in a row, they might have even sent someone around to check on him, but now they didn't really seem to care. Still, if the cithians found the discarded shell and the human clothing, wouldn't they come looking for the person who had been inside the shell? And if they did, might one of them remember that there was one human who had not turned up for his food on that day?

Denny sat down on the floor next to the maton and leaned back against the wall. He touched the silver ball with the toe of his shoe, moving it slowly across the thin rug. When Loma had told him about the maton, it had seemed very important that he find one, but now that he had it, he wasn't sure what to do next. Loma had said there was a lot more in the memory than the pictures of the sick people. He supposed Athena was part of that "lot more." Maybe she was all of it. To Denny, it seemed impossible that something like Athena could fit into the little cube of memory, much less leave room for other things.

He gave the little ball another soft kick and watched it wobble over the floor. He could pick it up, and maybe ask Athena what else was in there with her, but it would hurt again. And he would be tired. And...and...and...

Denny struggled up out of darkness and confusion. It took him a moment to realize that he had fallen asleep and the lights had turned themselves off. He raised up on one elbow and waved his other arm to make the light wake up. The yellowish glow sputtered into life. For a moment, he couldn't think what had pulled him out of sleep, then there was a rap at the door.

"Denny?" said a muffled voice. "Are you all right?"

He struggled to his feet, still feeling a deep ache in both his hands and his legs. He meant to open the door and step out, but he'd barely palmed the lock before the door swung open and Sirah stepped inside. Her lips were pressed together firmly, and she had an expression on her face that reminded Denny of Auntie Talla. "What happened? Are you okay?"

"Nothing happened." Denny rubbed at his eyes. "I just fell asleep."

Cousin Yulia appeared at the door and looked past Sirah's shoulder. "Is he all right?" she asked, as if Denny had never spoken at all.

Sirah still had her eyes fixed on Denny's face. "He says he's fine," she said, "but he doesn't look fine." She stepped aside to let Yulia in. Now they were both standing in Denny's front room, staring at Denny.

Denny suddenly felt both a little angry and a lot embarrassed. Angry, because neither of the two girls seemed to be listening to him. Embarrassed, because no one had been in his compartment in a long time, not since all the way back to when his father had been consigned. It wasn't that Denny was embarrassed because the room was so messy. Really it wasn't. He was embarrassed because the room, the whole compartment, was so empty. Everything Denny owned, everything but the rest of his father's statues, were gone.

Still, neither Yulia nor Sirah said a thing about the compartment as they came inside. Yulia spotted the maton on the floor and immediately walked over to look down at it. Sirah only kept looking at Denny so hard that it made Denny feel uncomfortable.

"What's wrong?" he said.

Sirah tilted her head to the side and continued to study him. "That's what I want to know. You look sick."

"Well, I'm not sick. I'm okay. Really."

Yulia reached down to pick up the maton. "How does this..."

Denny jumped quickly to get between her and the silver ball. "You have to be careful," he said.

"I'm not going to break it," Yulia said.

"It's not that. It's..." Denny shrugged. "When you touch it, it kind of hurts."

"Hurts?" She looked past Denny at the small device. "Like tingles?"

"Like hurts," said Denny. "Really hurts." He leaned over and picked up the maton, being careful to keep the scrap of cloth wrapped around it. He tried to remember what the voice had said the first time he touched the maton. "It's a...noodle interest?" He shrugged again. "Something like that."

Yulia's forehead creased in puzzlement. "Noodle?" She shook her head. "I don't know what that means."

Sirah finally stopped looking at Denny long enough to look at the little ball in his hand. The look she gave the silver thing was no nicer than the one she had been giving Denny. "If it hurts, are you sure you're using it right?"

"Yes," said Denny. "I mean...I think so."

Yulia bit her lip. "Maybe I should try it."

Denny nodded slowly. There was no reason he could think of to keep Yulia from using the maton, but something made him feel like he shouldn't. "Maybe I should ask," he said.

"Ask who?"

"Athena."

Both Yulia and Sirah looked at him with puzzled expressions. "Who?"

"Athena. She's..." Denny searched for the right words, and realized he didn't know or couldn't remember the right words to tell them what Athena was. He took a deep breath. "Wait a minute."

Slowly, he started to retell the events of the previous day, starting with putting on the disguise and walking through the city to the domed building. Sirah seemed to be shocked at what he had done, and even Yulia's eyes were wide as Denny talked about going into the building and talking to the unseen voice. As he talked Denny first leaned against the wall, then slowly lowered himself to the floor. By the time he finished telling them about using Athena's directions to escape the building, all three of them were sitting on the thin rug.

Sirah had her hands locked tightly together and a horrified expression on her face. "Denny! I can't...I mean, you... What if you'd been caught?"

Denny shrugged. "They would probably have just consigned me. And we're all about to be consigned anyway."

"You don't know that," said Sirah. She scooted toward him, her knees wrinkling the surface of the rug. "They could have done anything."

"Well, I didn't get caught."

The answer didn't seem to make Sirah any happier. "Yet," was all she said.

Cousin Yulia had moved to lean against the opposite wall, but her eyes were still fixed on the little sphere in Denny's hand. "Every time you use the maton, it hurts," she said.

Denny looked away from Sirah and nodded. "A lot."

"And if you keep using it?"

"The big pain stops, but after a while you start getting tired. Athena says that it can cause..." Denny stopped, both because he couldn't remember the green woman's exact words, and because using the maton to get home didn't really seem to have made him sick. Not so sick that a little rest couldn't handle it. "Well, it makes you really tired. You're not supposed to use it too much."

Yulia nodded. "That sounds like a really good reason that more than one person should use it."

"I don't..."

She held out her hand. "You need to share the burden. Take turns. Let me try it."

Denny frowned, but after a moment he handed over the maton, still being careful to keep it wrapped in the bit of old shirt. "It really hurts. You might want to--"

Before he could finish the sentence, Yulia flipped back the cloth, reached down, and grabbed the silver ball firmly in her left hand. At once, her eyes flew open wide and her back arched. Her lips peeled back from her teeth. Her nostrils flared. Then it was over, and she relaxed, breathing hard.

Cousin Sirah slid around on the rug until she was sitting beside Denny, both of them facing toward Yulia. "Are you all right?"

Yulia took a moment to respond, but eventually she nodded. "I don't... No, wait." Her mouth turned up in a sudden smile. "Hello, Athena!"

Denny looked around the room for the green woman, but without the maton in hand, there was nothing to see. "Is she talking to you?"

Yulia nodded. Her eyes were fixed on a point in the center of the room. "Yes, hold on... She's telling me..." Yulia's head slowly turned from left to right, as if she was watching someone walk across the room. "Yes," she said. Then after a pause, "yes," again.

"What's she doing?" asked Sirah.

"She can see Athena. We can't." Denny leaned forward. It was strange to watch Yulia talk to someone that was invisible to the rest of them. He found himself wishing he was the one talking to Athena. "Can you ask her if the cithians found the things I left by the dome?"

Yulia nodded without looking his way. "Athena, did the cithians... Wait." Her eyes flicked down toward Denny. "She can hear you, you just can't hear her. She says yes, the cithians found the stuff."

Now Denny really did feel sick. He hadn't expected the remains of his disguise to be found so quickly. "Do they know a human left them?"

There was a short delay before Yulia answered. "She's not sure." Another pause. "Athena only knows the things that the cithians have put into their central, um, central store. Somebody may know it was a human, but they haven't recorded it."

Sirah rocked forward, sitting on her knees. "You can really see someone?"

Yulia nodded. "A woman, just like Denny said, only she's not made of stone."

"She's not?"

"It's more like, like skin. Like she's real."

Denny wondered if Yulia was seeing the same thing he had. Maybe Athena had changed her appearance. Maybe she was different for everybody.

Yulia suddenly broke into a wide smile. "She knows my name."

Denny remembered when Athena had first spoken to him. "She knew mine too."

Sirah scooted forward again. "What about me? Does she know my name?"

Yulia looked at the center of the room, frowned, then turned to Sirah. "She says she does, but she has it wrong. She says your name is Ani... Anisyretta."

Cousin Sirah's mouth flew open. "It is!" she said. "That's the name my mother gave me. The name I used before—" She swallowed hard, then turned to look at Denny. "Sirah is just a nickname."

Denny was amazed to hear it. Sirah had always just been Sirah. Athena didn't just know how to find her way out of cithian buildings, she knew other things. Secret things. He grinned. "Athena," he said. "Do you know where to find some powdermilk?" he asked.

"Or crackers!" added Sirah. "Or..."

Yulia held up a finger to signal silence. "She says that human food...stuff? Foodstuff. Anyway, human food is kept in a building called maxillary two-fourteen."

"Where is—"

"She says it's just outside the gate."

Denny clapped his hands together. "Tomorrow we feast!"

Yulia's usual nervous look returned. "Do you think we should?"

"Why not?" Denny said with a shrug. "Athena got me through the big storage building without getting caught. I'll bet she can tell us how to get away with some stupid crackers."

"Maybe," said Sirah. "But if there's human food missing from storage, won't the cithians know it was taken by humans?"

Denny had to admit that they would. "But what about something else? Athena knows about everything. What would you want if you could have anything?"

Sirah was slow to answer, but Yulia's face suddenly lit up. "I know what we should ask." She pulled in a deep breath and turned to the open space at the center of the room where the woman only she could see was standing. "Athena, do you know where we are going to be consigned? Will it be the same place as my parents?"

Denny found himself looking at the empty air, as if expecting an answer. It was only when he heard a strange sound, a sound not too far from a moan, that he looked back at Yulia. Her mouth was open. Her lip trembling.

"But..." she said. "No, but..."

Then she started to scream.

21

Yulia hurled the maton across the room with enough force to leave a dent in the thin wall of Denny's compartment. The silver ball fell to the floor, bounced, and rolled in a lopsided path to clink loudly into the side of one of his father's metal scuptures.

"No!" Yulia shouted, her voice coming out with a raw force that sounded as if it would tear her throat. "She's lying!"

Sirah scrambled to her feet and rushed toward Yulia, but the other girl turned away from her, facing into the wall and throwing her arms over her head. "No," she said. "No." Her voice was muffled behind her hair and her arms, but it was still painfully ragged. After a moment, her back heaved up and down, and Denny heard her words turn into sobs.

"Did it hurt you?" asked Sirah. She pulled one of Yulia's hands away from her face and tugged open her fingers to look at her palm, as if expecting to see painful burns. Yulia only continued to sob.

Denny looked down at the maton. The silver surface still had prints showing on the surface from where Yulia's hand had been wrapped around it. He reached down and picked it up.

At once the pain ripped through him head to toe. If anything, it seemed worse than before. He had just enough time to think that if it went on any longer, it would kill him. Then the pain was gone and Athena was standing beside Yulia.

As Yulia had said, Athena no longer looked like she was made of stone. Or at least, not completely. The woman's robe now looked as if it was made from a pale cloth that bunched and hung against her legs. Her hair, pulled tightly behind her head, was a glossy black. Her skin was, kind of like skin, only she seemed milky pale. A color that Denny had never seen on a real human.

"Athena?"

The woman turned toward him. Despite how real the rest of her looked, her eyes were still as featureless and smooth as stone. Across the room, Yulia was still crying, but Athena's face was touched by the same slight smile that had been there since Denny first saw her. "Hello again, Denning."

"What did you tell Yulia?"

Athena tipped her head to one side. "She was asking about other humans."

Denny looked across the room toward Yulia. Touching the maton hurt, but Yulia had felt that pain like he had, and she hadn't screamed, or cried. Something that Athena had said had hurt her more than the agony that came from the machine. There was something here, a danger that Denny didn't fully understand, but one that he also couldn't avoid. "Yes," he said.

Athena looked at him with her stony eyes and her slight smiled. "I told her there were twelve."

"Twelve?"

"Twelve humans."

Denny took a moment to think, then nodded slowly. "In Jukal."

"Yes," said Athena. "Twelve humans in the Human Containment Facility, Jukal Plex, Rask."

There was nothing wrong with what she said, but Denny still found that there was a tightness squeezing at his stomach, and a cold feeling in his arms and legs. "But that's just in Jukal. There are other towns."

"Yes," said Athena. "There are eight major complexes on each of the three major continents, each of them arranged to mimic the placement of limbs around the body of a cithian adult," said Athena. From somewhere, a simulated wind seemed to ruffle her simulated hair. "There are 432 smaller communities, chiefly on the southernmost continent."

Denny found he had to clear his throat before asking, "...and how many humans?"

"Twelve," said Athena, her smile still the same. "There are twelve humans in the Human Containment Facility, Jukal Plex."

"And in other complexes?"

"There are no humans in other complexes," said the woman who wasn't there. "There are no other humans anywhere. There are only twelve."

22

Denny's tongue felt thick in his mouth. He was about to ask something more when an idea occurred to him. "You're wrong."

Athena didn't change her expression, but there was a quick blink of her center less eyes. "In what way?"

"There are thirteen people in Jukal," he said. With every word, he felt a little better. It was obvious Athena didn't know everything after all. If she could miss a human who was right here in the city, how could she know about people scattered around the world? "You forgot Loma."

"Paloma Azi," said Athena. "Was consigned on Tollsday, cycle 14, 237 PC."

"She was consigned?" The date Athena gave was the same as the last day Denny had seen Loma. They must have come for her right after Denny had left. "Consigned where?"

"The Jukal Plex Human Containment Facility is the terminal node."

Denny had never heard this phrase before, and he wanted to reply that he didn't know what Athena meant. But he did. He really did. "They killed her."

"Yes."

"And my father?"

"Carrel Ellitson was consigned on Passday, cycle 22, 234 PC." Athena never stopped smiling.

"Consigned...where?"

"The Jukal Plex Human Containment Facility is the terminal node."

Denny didn't notice that he was falling until his knees came down hard against the floor. There was pain, but that seemed like a distant thing. Across the room, Yulia was saying something to Sirah, but that might have been something happening in another compartment, in another building, in another plex, on a different planet. Sirah turned toward him and took a step, but slowly... everything was moving so slowly.

On the floor, the little metal figure his father had made still sat in its usual place, with its tiny metal fist raised above its head, and its tiny metal body caught in middle of a motion Denny couldn't name. He had always thought that one day he would be able to give the metal figure back to his father. Then his father would know that Denny remembered him, had waited to be with him, had thought about him. But now the metal things—the little figure, the curved shapes that stood beside the bed, the taller, jangly piece sat in the far corner—they were all there was. All that was left of his father.

Denny wished that he had never sold one of the pieces to Poppa Jam, never bought the shell and the heavy cloth for his disguise, never taken the maton. Never talked to Old Loma. He wished that the chug had never dropped its awful little purpley cube into his box. If none of that had happened, Denny's father would still be dead, but at least Denny wouldn't know.

Something moved in front of him. Denny's eyes seemed to have a hard time focusing. "Denny?" A voice. Sirah's voice.

"We're all that's left," he said. "Just us."

"I know," said Sirah. Her voice was raw. "Yulia said the same thing. But there's something else we need to worry about."

Denny blinked. He realized that his eyes were full of tears. "How can there be anything else?"

"It's what Omi said. Do you remember? Last week at Restaurant."

It was hard to think, but Denny dragged his mind back to Omi—silly Omi and his plastic shell, Omi who had always liked human music and human dancing and human food. Moments before, it had been the world that seemed to run slowly, but now it was Denny's mind. Just thinking of something other than the words Athena had just said to him was like lifting something very heavy.

"Omi said... he said." And then he remembered. That tight feeling came back to his guts. "He said we were all going to be consigned."

Sirah nodded. "He said we were all going to be consigned *soon.*"

23

Denny took the ground transport to the spaceport. At first the little stop by the quarter was empty, and when the first transport stopped Denny stepped inside and took a spot near the viewport at the front of the pod. At the last minute, just as the transport was about to leave, a cithian male hurried down the ramp and slipped through the doors. He turned his broad eye pads toward Denny, clearly expecting him to get up and leave.

Denny stayed in his seat.

The cithian thumped one of its clangers against the thick side of its heavy shell. Denny noticed that the shell was notched at several points. If he thought about it, he could have probably figured out the cithian's rank. He didn't try.

The clangers sounded again as the doors of the train slid closed and the little compartment began to move. In the enclosed space, the sound of the cithian's warning rose from a rapid pounding into a buzz that made Denny's ears ache. The cithian stepped toward him. Denny knew that the cithan was much stronger than him. The manipulators on the heavy forelimbs could have thrown him across the car. The razor edges of its mid-limbs could slash at him. Could kill him. Denny stayed in his seat.

The cithian loomed over him, close enough that Denny could see the bright light of Whetsday shining through the translucent red-black edges of its shell. Close enough to smell its powdery, sweetish smell. Then the big male backed away. It moved to the rear half of the pod and settled onto the cithian-sized bench. "Where is your respect?" the cithian asked.

Denny didn't reply.

24

By the time Denny reached the spaceport, the two suns were touching. Under his feet the sidewalk was so hot that it burned through the soles of his shoes and his shadow was touched by purplish fringes. As he approached the door of the port, Denny wished that he was not alone. This would have been much easier if Sirah or Yulia had been with him. But Yulia had gone to tell those who were there at the compartment buildings–Auntie Flash, Poppa Gow, Nonni Hanti, Auntie Yue and Auntie Fro. Sirah had gone to the market to find Auntie Talla. If she got back in time, she would also be the one to tell Poppa Jam and Cousin Haw–if they told them at all.

Back at Denny's compartment, when Athena's words were still sinking in, they had argued about who to tell. Sirah had said that they needed to tell everyone, right away. It was only fair to warn people about what was really coming.

Yulia has said they shouldn't tell anyone, because the cithians might learn that they knew. Besides, she said, there was nothing they could do. If they were all about to be consigned, better everyone didn't know what that meant. It would only make everyone upset.

Despite how much Denny might have wished that he didn't know himself, he had eventually agreed with Sirah. If they were all going to be consigned–*killed,* consigned meant killed–in just a few days, then there was really nothing to be afraid of. If the cithians found out that Denny had gone to their storage facility and taken a maton, if they found out he knew things he shouldn't know...they might take him away sooner, but it would not be all that much sooner. In the end, he just couldn't imagine not telling everyone. If they said nothing, there would be people boxing up their things on consignment day, hoping to see long missing parents, or children, or spouses. Denny didn't think he could stand by and watch them, knowing how it was all going to end.

Denny paused only a moment at the door of the spaceport. Outside it was hot and the light of the two suns seemed ready to set his hair on fire, but at least the air wasn't too bad. He took a deep breath, and plunged inside.

Inside, it was so much cooler that Denny shivered. Even before he took a breath, the sharp tang of ammonia bit at his nose. He knew it was only a tiny amount, just enough to flavor the air for those races that really needed it, but almost immediately Denny's eyes began to water and his nose began to run. He didn't know how Kettle could stand working in this place all day.

He passed a pair of skynx talking together near the door. Like skynx everywhere, they pretty much ignored him. The same could not be said of the dasiks. Denny was only a dozen steps inside the building before a lesser dasik appeared. Its long face had the same no-expression as every other dasik, but the way it held one long clawed hand near a stunstik across its chest, made the creature's mood pretty clear. It tapped a button that said, "State your business."

"I need to talk to Kettle."

The long finger tapped again. "This statement was not understood."

"Cousin Kettle," said Denny. He paused to cough as the bitter air burned in his throat. "The human who works here."

The dasik clicked its teeth together. "Boarding area three," said the little talking button on the dasik's jacket.

Denny slipped around the dasik. Each of the boarding areas was lined with cushioned benches. In the first area, a pair of klickiks were sprawled on the benches, apparently asleep. The second area was empty. In the third area, three skynx were waiting. One of them had a water bottle that he used to spray himself with a mist. The other two looked miserable.

Do they know? Denny wondered. Did every cithian, every skynx, every person of every race, know that there were only a few humans left? Did they have a part in it?

On the other side of the waiting skynx, Denny saw Cousin Kettle. Kettle was pushing a low cart stacked with boxes. From the way Kettle moved, Denny could tell the boxes were heavy.

Kettle pushed the cart up to the three and stopped. For several seconds, he just stood there. Finally, one of the skynx, the one with the water bottle, fished in a small pouch and came out with a green token. It flipped the token toward Kettle, who caught it out of the air.

"Thank you," he said. Kettle had just started to turn away, when he saw Denny. At once, a frown settled over Kettle's face. He folded his arms across his chest. "The day is barely started," he said. "If you want to ride home with me, you've got a long wait."

Denny shook his head. "That's not why I'm here about."

Kettle turned, looking back up the hall toward the second area where one of the dasiks was standing. "It will have to wait. You're going to get me in trouble."

"We're kind of already in trouble," said Denny. "All of us."

"Earth, Denny." Kettle's frown deepened. "What did you do?"

"It's not me, it's..." Denny glanced at the trio of skynx. One of them had raised it low head. Its big, slitted eyes were looking their way. Maybe the skynx knew they were the last few humans, and that the last few were about to be killed. Maybe they didn't. In either case, it seemed important that the skynx not know that the humans knew. Denny took Kettle by the arm and drew him toward the corner of the loading area. They went only a few steps before Kettle wrenched his arm free.

"What's going on?"

Denny opened his mouth to tell him, then realized that he didn't know where to start. He couldn't think of anything to say, any place to begin, that didn't sound ridiculous. Finally, he decided that there was nothing to do but charge straight in. "They're going to kill us."

"Who is?"

Denny took a quick look over his shoulder. How good was skynx' hearing? "The cithians," he said quietly.

Kettle rolled his eyes. "What did you do this time? Did you grab extra chez at line-up?"

"It's nothing like that. Nothing I did." Except, of course, for disguising himself as a moltling, sneaking into a cithian storehouse and sneaking off with a maton, but Denny didn't want to get into that. "I mean they're really, really going to kill us. Actually kill us. Dead. The cithians."

Kettle's angry expression tipped towards confusion. "What are you talking about?"

"It's when we're consigned," said Denny. "They don't actually send us to another place like they've always said.

They just...they..." Thoughts of his father rushed in again, and Denny found he had to sniff back tears. Then he realized that he was crying in front of Kettle and he turned away, wiping at his eyes with the back of his arm. "They just kill us. Kill everybody."

"Who told you that?" asked Kettle. "Somebody is lying to you."

Denny started to answer, then only shrugged. "They're not. I wish it was a lie, but it's real. Only it's kind of a long story."

Kettle stared over his shoulder. "I can't talk any more right now. Go outside. Wait for me."

Looking back, Denny saw that two of the dasiks were approaching. One of them was the one Denny had met near the door. His long, clawed fingers were again lingering near his stunstik.

All of the skynx raised their heads to look at him as Denny went past. One of the dasiks pressed the button that said "leave this area immediately," but Denny was already past him before the button was through. He was almost to the door when a deep, buzzing voice spoke from his right.

"This is the one," it said. "Human!"

Denny stopped and turned. The two klickiks were looking at him. With their hard shiny faces and hard shiny eyes, Denny couldn't read their expressions, but they held their manipulator arms high in a way he knew meant they were interested in something.

"Yes?" said Denny.

"You are the one." The klickik raised and lowered its crest then flicked a red arm toward the door to the sidewalk. "You are the human who dances."

"Yes."

"Do this," said the klickik. "Do the human dancing." One of its other arms dipped down into a pouch in the side of its body and came back up immediately. It flipped a small collection of green tokens that landed on the hard floor by Denny's feet.

He was sure then. He was sure that all of them, every traveler coming through the spaceport, every cithian in the plex, every skynx or chug or klickik. Everyone everywhere. They knew that they humans were down to a tiny few, and that soon they would be gone. The klickik wanted him to dance, because it didn't want to miss its last chance to see a human doing a human thing.

Denny had never felt less like dancing. Under the hard stare of the klickik's huge silvery eyes, he found that his own eyes were leaking again. Tears were running down his cheek, dripping from the point of his chin. Some of it was the bitter air inside the space port. Most of it wasn't. Denny didn't bother to wipe the tears away.

Slowly, he started to move his feet. Slower still, he started to wave his arms.

"Home," he sang. "Chariot take me home." And he danced. "Grace, how sweet the sound."

25

It was much later, after the two suns had come apart and Denny once again had a pair of different colored shadows, when Kettle came out of the spaceport. Denny had expected him to be angry. To show up with his arms folded and his face screwed up in that "you're embarrassing me" look. But Kettle came through the foggy doors of the port and walked straight up to him.

"This is real, isn't it?" he asked.

Denny nodded. And then, starting with the chug and his little purple cube, Denny told Cousin Kettle everything that had happened.

When he was done, the two of them sat on the sidewalk, beside the row of dots that led to the ground transport, and stared at the hot ground. Some cithians passed by, and a group of skynx, but no one asked Denny to dance. Which was good.

Finally, after a long silence, Kettle stood up and brushed his hands across the back of his uniform pants. He had said nothing about Denny's story, and he still didn't. But it was obvious he believed it all. "I have to go inside. There's a cargo shuttle to load."

Denny stood and nodded. "I guess I'll go back to the quarter."

Kettle started to turn, then turned back. "You want to come with me?" He shrugged. "I suppose it doesn't really matter if the dasiks are mad at me now."

Together they walked back into the port and Denny winced again at the bite of ammonia in the air. Kettle saw him blinking and gave a quick laugh. "You get used to it."

No I won't, thought Denny. *There's no time to get used to anything.* But he didn't say that aloud.

They went past the first four waiting areas. This late in the day, all but one of the bays were empty. In that one, a tight group of cithians were sitting together. Denny thought one of them might have been the big male he upset in the transport pod, but if he was, the cithian didn't say anything as they went past.

In the fifth area, there were a dozen of the little carts like the one Kettle had been pushing earlier. "Help me with this, and we'll both leave when it's done."

Denny helped Kettle attach three of the carts together, like a little train, then they pulled them out onto the hot tarmac. A shuttle waited, no more than a hundred steps or so from the doors. As they got closer, Denny realized the ships were much larger than he had thought. The doors at the base of the shuttle were big enough to drive three road ferries through, side by side. The room beyond those doors would have held a whole floor of Denny's compartment building, and had space for another floor above that. There were already many boxes and containers stacked in the big room when they came up the ramp with the short train of carts. Kettle called a halt in the middle of the space and directed Denny in where they should stack the contents.

Above them, ramps and walkways extended into the gloom.

"Does the pilot sit up there?" asked Denny.

Kettle shook his head. "There is no pilot." He lifted a heavy box, turned around, and sat it on top of another. "These things aren't like picture book space ships. They're just shuttles."

"But who flies it?"

"There's a kind of maton," said Kettle. "You tell it where you want to go, and it goes." He shrugged. "They're all pretty much the same."

Denny stepped away from the supplies and walked over to the bottom of the nearest ramp. He could see that there were lights up there. Some kind of rooms. "Where does it go?"

"Anywhere. See this is really only half a shuttle. Not even that much." Kettle held his hands up together. "The two parts fly together between planetary systems. Then, when they get close to where they are going." He took one hand and slowly lowered it. "This part drops off and lands, leaving the star drive–which is really the bigger part–in orbit."

Denny had seen a thousand shuttles come and go, and seen people from many worlds walk past. "Kettle, where can this thing go?"

"Anywhere," said Kettle. Then he looked at Denny, and Denny looked back, and for the first time that day, he smiled.

26

PASSDAY

On Passday, Denny had a surprise, attended a funeral, and started a rebellion.

Hiser Grismalamacata Omicradiscrad, Overcontroller Human Assistance Authority, came into the gather room when Restaurant was almost over. There were four dasiks with him, and all of them had thick cylinders grasped in their long, clawed fingers. Denny had never seen anything like the cylinders before.

The big cithian pushed through the blue door without speaking. He crossed the room with his hard feet clacking on the floor, moving past the tables where Auntie Yue and Auntie Fro and Nonni Hacci watched him with barely concealed nervousness. Past Poppa Gow in his wheeled chair. Past the tall table where Cousin Haw sat scowling beside Poppa Jam. Past Denny and Kettle and Auntie Flash and Yulia. Past the stove where Auntie Talla and Sirah were working.

The humans had all decided to come to Restaurant. They did it partly because, after doing the same thing for so many weeks, the cithians would expect them to be in the gather room. If they were not there...well, none of them knew what would happen. They were also there because Restaurant was where they met, where they talked. Auntie Talla hosted Restaurant, and did the cooking, but really it was something that they did together. If they were going to make a decision, this seemed like the place it should be done. But they had not expected the cithians to move so quickly.

Overcontoller Hiser stood in the center of the room, his bulk resting on the dark jointed claws of his rear limbs, and slowly raised himself. The deep notches along the edges his shell, the mark of both his age and rank within the Plex, glowed red under the lights. The blunt knobs of his clangers thumped a loud call for attention. "Humans," he said. "This is a special day."

We've waited too late, thought Denny. *We're all being consigned tonight. We're all being consigned right now.*

Hiser lifted one hooked forelimb and signaled to the dasiks. Each of them advanced, holding the cylinders in front of their narrow chests. There was a faint mist coming from each of the cylinders, like steam, but this was a strange heavy kind of steam that didn't rise, but fell toward the floor. Maybe they were not going to even bother pretending to consign the humans. Maybe they were going to kill them right here, in the gather room. And why not? Who was there left to fool?

Denny's mouth was dry. There was a sharp, bitter taste and his blood pounded in his ears. His stomach knotted, though he was surprised to find that he was not really afraid. He was angry. He glanced over at Sirah. She was watching the dasiks approach. Everyone was watching the dasiks, even Overcontroller Hiser.

There was a knife on the table next to Denny. Not a little knife, but a big, ragged-edged blade that Auntie Talla used for cutting the meat before it went on her stove. Denny set his hand on the table next to the blade. Dasiks were much stronger than people, and their hides were supposed to be very tough—stronger than metal, some people said. He moved his finger closer to the blade. Probably if Denny tried to attack one of the dasiks, he wouldn't even hurt it. Probably he would just get killed. But maybe not. His fingers closed around the knife.

Besides, Denny wasn't angry at the dasiks. Dasiks only did what other people told them. It was the cithians. His grip on the blade tightened. The cithians who had pretended to be their friends. The cithians who kept them prisoner, generation after generation. The cithians who killed them one by one, year after year, decade after decade. The cithians who had killed his father.

He slid the knife from the table, testing its weight. The Overcontroller was maybe three steps away. No matter how fast the dasiks were, no matter what kind of weapons they were carrying, Denny could cross that space before they could stop him. Even cithians had soft places.

A new figure came through the blue door. Another cithian. It moved quickly into the room. This cithian was not as large as Hiser, but where the Overcontroller was old and bulky, this cithian was sleek and fast. Its reddish shell was barely wider than its body, the spikes and edges of its mid-limbs razor sharp. It advanced straight toward Denny.

Then the cithian's mouthparts rose in a kind of smile. "Denny!" he said. "Did you try the izycrem?"

Even then it took Denny a moment to recognize the newcomer. "Omi?"

The young cithian hurried up to Denny's table, hooked one forelimb over the back of a chair, and pulled it out. He settled his gleaming new shell onto the chair. The heavy cloth wrappings and the plastic cover of a moltling were gone. Omi was all gleaming dark red shell and hard new limbs. "Denny. Did you eat the izycrem?"

He doesn't know. The knife in Denny's hand felt suddenly hot. He can't know.

Denny was so focused on Omi, that he jumped when one if the dasiks dropped a cylinder on the table with a thump. Close up, the cylinder seemed to be spotted with frost, like the frost that spotted the ground sometimes on Dimsday.

"My second has given away the surprise," said the Overcontroller. "We found this special human food in our supplies. This seemed a good time to distribute this special food."

Denny had never heard of izycrem, but he could see that some of the older humans were familiar with it. Auntie Yue was already tugging at the top of the cylinder the dasiks had placed on her table.

"Why?" said Denny.

The Overcontroller tilted its eyepads toward him. "Why?"

"Why was this a good time?"

The question seemed to take the cithian by surprise. He raised a mid-limb and scratched at the circle of heavy plate beneath his head. "There is...some chance that the human population of Jukal Plex will be relocated in the next few cycles."

Omi turned his head in a way that Denny recognized as an expression of surprise. "I thought it was this cycle. I thought–"

The Overcontroller raised both forelimbs. "Let us leave the humans to their treat. We have other things to do,"

Omi got out of his chair. "But I didn't have any izycrem." The Overcontroller kept walking. Omi turned his eyepads back toward the cylinder on the table, gave his clangers a little riff of irritation, and followed the Overcontroller back through the blue door. The dasiks followed behind them. Soon enough, there were only humans in the room.

With a pop, Auntie Yue succeeded in wrestling the top from one of the cylinders. She reached inside with a froon, and dug out something that was a kind of yellowish-white paste. Auntie Fro eagerly took a slab of the stuff on her plate. Others were raising their plates and coming to her.

Sirah grabbed the top of the cylinder in front of Denny and gave it a tug. The material inside was a different color than in the one Auntie Yue had opened. A kind of pale reddish tan color. Waves of deep cold seemed to come from the cylinder as Sirah dragged a froon across the surface, sliced off a curling mass of the material, and transferred it to a plate.

Denny slowly removed the knife from below the table, raised it up, turned it over in his hand, and placed it down on the table in front of him. He could see Sirah looking at him. He felt like he had done something wrong, but he didn't know if it was picking up the knife, or not using the knife, that was bothering him.

A plate slid in front of him, weighted with a fist-sized chunk of the izycrem. "Try it," said Sirah.

Denny looked at the lump of unfamiliar food. It was starting to melt around the sides, tan drops streaming into a puddle on the plate. "I don't think I want it," he said.

Sirah plunged her froon into the melting mass, scooped a bit, and pushed it toward Denny. "Try it," she said again, more insistently.

"Why?"

She shrugged. "Because, no matter what happens next, you'll probably never get another chance. Because tomorrow, we could both be dead."

Denny thought about that a moment. He opened his mouth. Sirah pushed the froonful of tan stuff in. It was shockingly cold against his teeth. Denny was sure he'd never eaten anything nearly so cold before. But as the stuff melted against his tongue, it changed, unfolding into new textures and a great wash of flavor. It filled his mouth with a taste that was so different from anything he'd had before that it made him actually sway in his seat.

"It's really good," he said, around his slightly numbed tongue.

Sirah smiled at him. She put the froon into her own mouth and licked off the remainder. "Some things still are."

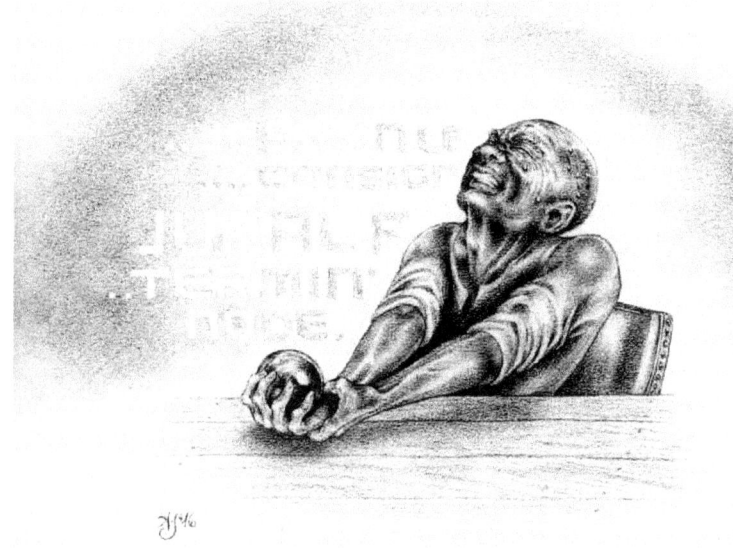

27

After the izycrem had been reduced to a few gooey puddles in the bottoms of the cylinders, all the humans in the human quarter of Jukal Plex–which, if Athena were right, was every human everywhere–settled down to talk. Auntie Talla had heated her big domed stove, and was cooking circles of flat bread to hand out, just to give people something to chew on. Kettle had positioned himself near the big blue door that the cithians used, just in case Overcontroller Hiser or Omi decided to come back unexpectedly.

By now, everyone knew what Denny and Yulia had learned. Most of them had heard it more than once. But still Denny found himself standing near the center of the room, repeating the story of the chug, and the storehouse, and Athena over and over. Sirah stood with him, joining in now and then as people around the room asked questions. Yulia added her comments occasionally, but now that everyone was together, she seemed uncomfortable about being at the focus of attention. Denny didn't blame her.

"This can't be right," said Nonni Hacci. Her voice was thin, and the look on her face confused. "Consigning doesn't mean killing."

"Of course not," said Autie Yue. "We've all been consigned." Auntie Fro nodded in agreement.

"This is different," said Denny. "This is..." He paused to think of the words that Athena had used. "This is the terminal...the last place. When people are moved here, they don't get consigned somewhere else."

For a long, uncomfortable moment, everyone was quiet. They had been to this point before. They kept coming back to this point. No one seemed to know how to move to the next thing, how to keep the discussion from circling round, and round, and round. They'd never had to face anything like this. For as long as Denny knew, and probably as long as anyone else in the room knew, human beings had never had to make any decision as a group. If you wanted to make Restaurant, you did that. If you wanted a store, then you did that. If you wanted to dance, you danced. But the things that affected them all–food, water, the compartment buildings where they lived–all those things came from someone else, from the cithians.

It was Poppa Gow who broke the silence. "Let us say you are right," he said. His voice was soft as dry leaves. Despite spending years and years at Jukal Plex, he still had a strange way of talking. Something left over from the place he had lived long ago, as a child. He raised a hand with fingers small as twigs. "I am not saying you are correct," he added, "but let us...pretend? Yes, let us pretend that you are. What would you have us do then?"

Kettle answered from his place near the door. "We take a shuttle."

"Take a shuttle," said Poppa Jam. Just the way the man said those three words, made them seem like the most ridiculous thing ever said in all the worlds. At Jam's elbow, Cousin Haw gave a nasal snort of laughter. "Take a shuttle and go where?"

"I don't know," admitted Kettle.

Jam looked at Kettle for a few seconds longer, then turned his face toward Denny. "And how about you?" he asked. "Do you know where we're going?"

Denny looked at Poppa Gow hopefully, but the old man seemed lost in thought, as if the single question had exhausted him. "Away," he said. "That's all that matters. We have to go away. And quickly."

"I don't see why," said Nonni Hacci. "This is our home."

"We've all been consigned before," said Auntie Yue. Auntie Fro nodded.

And here we are again, thought Denny. Back where we started. He closed his eyes, and tried to say it as simply as he knew how. "The Overcontroller says we're all going to be consigned. Probably in just a few days.

Athena says that when you are consigned from Jukal, it just means that you die. There are no more humans anywhere else. When we die, there will be no more humans."

It was the same thing that they had already been told, and again the whole room fell into an awkward silence. Poppa Gow's dry voice broke the logjam for a second time. "I think you are right," he said. "We must leave right away." The words brought a gasp from Auntie Yue and another confused expression from Nonni Hacci.

Auntie Flash, her voice reduced to a reedy quaver by her affliction, spoke up for the first time. "I agree," she said.

Poppa Jam made a backhanded wave. "Of course you do. It's your boy who came up with this spaceship nonsense."

"That's not–" Auntie Flash began, but Jam cut her off before she could get out any more.

"I can tell you this," the man said. "I'm not going anywhere that I don't want to go." Beside him, Cousin Haw folded his arms, giving the room the glare usually reserved for people suspected of taking something from Poppa Jam's store.

From across the room, a circle of browned flatbread arced down to strike Poppa Jam in the face with an audible slap. The big man's mouth opened in shock.

"Idiot," Auntie Talla shouted from her place by the stove. "If they come for you, how are you going to stop them?"

"Well..." said Poppa Jam. "Well...I'll pay them."

"Credits don't matter."

Jam drew himself up and faced her with a confident look. "Credits always matter."

It was Auntie Talla's turn to roll her eyes. "The cithians will just kill you and take all your credits. All your other things, too. They don't need to deal with you. They *own* you."

The idea seemed to offend Poppa Jam. He ground his teeth together hard enough that his lips puffed out. "You actually believe this? These..." he gestured toward Denny and Sirah. "Children."

For the first time, Denny felt a new kind of worry. "We're telling the truth."

"They are," Yulia added, speaking up from her seat next to Auntie Flash. "We are. I heard it from Athena myself."

"Athena." This time, Poppa Jam didn't just lace his voice with scorn, he smacked both hands against the table, making a slap so loud that Nonni Hacci jumped in her seat. "The ghost woman from a magic ball."

"It's not magic," Yulia said loudly. She rose halfway to her feet, then dropped back into her chair as faces turned her way. She glanced around and looked down, the floating weight of her curls half hiding her face. "It's a maton," she finished more softly.

"A maton," said Jam. "Which you know you're not supposed to have." He looked toward Denny. "Whatever it is, this thing is just showing you a story. Like a picture book."

"It's not like that." Denny searched for the words. "The cube, the one the chug gave me, it does have moving pictures—"

"See!" Jam looked at them all again. "See? This boy always has his face buried in some picture book. This story with us all being killed is like that. It's not real."

Across the room, Auntie Yue spoke up. "That must be it." Auntie Fro nodded.

All at once, it was if the whole room took a breath. Denny could see tightly clenched hands relax. Slumped shoulders rise. The sense of relief was so strong it was if someone had turned on a new set of lights.

"Just a story," said Nonni Hacci.

Denny looked at Sirah. She stared back. "Could it be?" She asked softly. "Could it not be true?"

"No. I wish it was only a story, but no."

Chairs scraped the floor. Poppa Jam was already on his feet. Cousin Haw right behind. "No, wait," said Denny, but everyone was talking now. Yue and Fro were moving to push Poppa Gow's chair. Yulia was shaking her head, but stayed slumped in her seat. "Wait," Denny tried again,

"Children can be so silly," said Nonni Hacci. Auntie Fro nodded.

A loud metallic clanging froze everyone in place. Auntie Talla stood behind her stove, her long curved stick in one hand. "All of you hush," she said firmly. Poppa Jam started to speak, but Talla cut him off with another sharp bang against the stove. "I've listened to Denny, and I've listened to Yulia, and I've listened to my own Sirah. I don't want to believe them any more than the rest of you do, but I didn't feed you people and take care of you all this time to watch you throw what's left of your lives away." She waved the curved stick toward the tables. "Sit down and listen."

Everyone but Poppa Jam obeyed quickly. Auntie Talla scowled at him. "So help me Jamison Leonard, you get in your chair, or you'll not get a bite of my food again, whether your life's short or long."

Poppa Jam sat, but the angry expression didn't leave his face. "You believe them? Have you even seen this maton they keep talking about?"

"No, but..."

"Where is it?" Jam spun toward Denny. "Show me this Athena."

Denny fished in his pocket and carefully drew out the little orb. He held it up, still wrapped in a bit of cloth torn from his shirt.

"Where's the magic woman?"

"You have to be touching it to see Athena," said Denny.

Jam wiggled his fingers. "Then bring it to me."

"It hurts when you touch it."

"You think I'm scared? Bring it here."

Denny took a reluctant step toward Jam's table. "Are you sure?"

Poppa Jam reached out and took the maton from Denny's hand. "How much does it hurt?"

"A lot. And you have to be careful not to hold it too long."

The store keeper folded back the cloth, looked at the silver curve of the maton for one long, silent second. Finally he blew his breath out in a loud, "Hmmph." Then he picked it up with his right hand. Immediately, Poppa Jam's face went rigid and his eyes bulged. Beads of sweat spread across his forehead. "I see her," he said. "I see..."

He rose up on his feet and slowly turned. Denny could see his eyes swiveling to follow an invisible form around the room. "You're wrong," he said. "You have to be wrong." The expression of anger slowly faded from Poppa Jam's face. His cheeks seemed to hollow out in an instant, his eyes looked sunken. His skin turned a weird shade of gray.

"Oh," he said. "Oh, Jessyn." Then Poppa Jam fell face down across the table and the silver ball fell from his hand.

Cousin Haw shot to his feet and backed away. Sirah rushed forward, putting her hand against Poppa Jam's throat. But Denny didn't have to wait for Sirah to say anything. He knew already.

Poppa Jam was dead.

28

They buried Poppa Jam in a little empty space between two of the compartment buildings. There was no cemetery in the quarter. Few people had died in Jukal in the past–if you didn't count all those who had been consigned–and always before those few who died had been turned over to the cithians. The cithians recycled their own dead. No one was sure what they did with the dead humans.

Denny had never even heard the word cemetery before. It was Poppa Gow who explained about cemeteries. About burying. There had been such a place back at Hanti Plex, many years before.

No one had suggested that they hand Poppa Jam's body over to the cithians. No one had suggested calling the Overcontroller, or any of the dasiks. Instead, they had taken the man's body carefully through the tight maze of buildings, to one of the few spots in the whole quarter where the ground was not paved. Then, using tools they took from Poppa Jam's own store, they dug a hole in the hard, gray, stony ground. Cousin Haw did most of the digging, when he wasn't crying. Then they put Poppa Jam in the hole. No one said anything. They didn't know what to say.

Denny wondered if all the people who were consigned, and the few who died, ended up in the same place. In his mind, he pictured a strange kind of cemetery, one with only one grave, and one big marker that said simply "Humans."

"What did he mean," Denny asked. "What's Jessyn?"

"Jamison's wife," said Auntie Talla. "She was consigned...well, before you were born."

Kettle looked at Denny as the others started to wander away. "What do we do now?" he asked.

Of all the things that had happened, Denny thought that one of the strangest was that Kettle was asking him what to do. "We leave," he said. "We talk to everyone again, and we get away, as fast as we can."

Together, Denny and Kettle helped Cousin Haw fill the hole.

29

Denny got off the lift at the very top floor, and pushed through the screen of leafy vines that drooped down over the wide door. The air up here was warm, damp, and carried the scents of soil and life. He squinted into the darkness. "Poppa Gow?"

Sometime, long before Denny was born, but after the population of the human quarter had started its long, steady drop, Poppa Gow had knocked down most of the walls on the top floor. Even after the accident had taken his legs, Gow had kept working in the building, reshaping it, changing the nest of tiny compartments into big, open spaces, and filling the area near the windows with pots, and troughs, and basins that supported many different kind of plants. The center of the floor was given over to winding paths that cut through areas filled with a plain gray mix of sand and gravel, most of it rubble from the buildings of the quarter–rotting bricks, bits of pavement, crumbling plaster. Somehow Poppa Gow had made the different shades of gray into twisting lines that sometimes turned into feathery mazes, sometimes into islands that rose up above surrounding sand. Denny never saw Gow working on this. How the man got through the sand in his wheeled chair, Denny didn't know.

Poppa Gow didn't answer his call, but eventually Denny found him anyway. The old man was near a window, holding up a plant with small pointy leafs. The brightness of Passday was fading, and at the moment all the plants looked to Denny as if they were flat black under the light of the red sun.

"Poppa Gow?" he tried again.

The man turned to him with a sad smile. "Hello, Denny. Did you finish with my old friend, Jam?"

"Yes. We..."

Gow raised a bony hand. "Please. It's enough to know he was cared for." He sat the plant down carefully on a small table, and lifted another pot, turning it back and forth as he inspected a small plant. "Did you know that Jam was older than me?"

Denny was surprised. "No."

"He was. Older than everyone except Loma." He put the second plant down and looked back at Denny. "I suppose that now I am the oldest. Maybe the oldest human in all the universe." His smile returned, not so sad this time. "And you are the youngest. That makes it very fit that you would come to see me."

Denny spotted a small stool between two nearby pots. He sat down carefully, not sure the stool would hold his weight. "I came to bring you back to Restaurant."

"But I am not hungry," said Poppa Gow.

"You don't have to eat, but we need to talk."

"Why?" He picked up a small pair of scissors and trimmed a tiny branch from the plant. "I think we have already decided what we are doing."

Denny slumped down, resting his arms on his knees. "I can't get Auntie Yue and Auntie Fro to come."

"I didn't expect they would." Poppa Gow turned the plant slowly around in his hands. "Probably they would not have come even if our friend Jam had not left us so suddenly."

"Nonni Hacci doesn't want to come either."

"Also expected."

"But if you tell them you are coming, then..."

"No," said Poppa Gow. He put the little plant back in its place and looked squarely at Denny. "I will not be going."

Denny felt an ache settle over his body. They hadn't even tried to get away, but already a third of the humans in Jukal were lost. Or dead. The whole idea of getting away felt both silly and hopeless.

Poppa Gow put a hand on Denny's shoulder. At first his touch was light, but his fingers gripped with surprising strength. "Don't think of this as a failure. After all, we wouldn't know what was happening if you had not told us."

"But does it matter?" asked Denny. "Even if we get away, there are so few of us."

"It would matter if there was only one," said Poppa Gow. He gave Denny's shoulder a final squeeze. "I think you already knew that."

30

SKIMSDAY

On Skimsday, Denny led an escape. He stood on the sidewalk outside the spaceport, near the place where he had danced so many times, and waited for the others to arrive. The low Skimsday suns made the spaceport seem like a different place, full of shadows and slowly shifting colors. There was also very little activity at the port today, only two shuttles coming in, and none scheduled to depart. Denny hoped they could change that schedule. One shuttle, headed out.

Down along the dotted line on the road, one ground transport arrived, and then another. The first of the day's scheduled shuttles descended on a tail of lightning and thunder. A few minutes later, Denny had to step aside so a crowd of cithians and a single tall, crested klickik could get from the doors of the port to the transport. He worried that the pods from the quarter might arrive while there were so many people there. Even one human drew a lot of attention out of the quarter. It would be hard to explain what seven of them were doing at the port together. But the next set of pods were also empty, and the cithians and the klickik left quickly. For several minutes after that, Denny worried that the transport from the quarter was taking too long to arrive, and that they would miss their chance.

Finally, the doors of two transport pods opened and humans poured out. Auntie Talla and Cousin Sirah were in the first pod with Auntie Flash. Auntie Talla was wearing the long robe Denny had seen her put on for trips to the market and carried a large rucksack in each hand. Cousin Sirah had her dark hair wrapped in a cloth, and a pack slung across her back. Auntie Flash seemed to be having trouble walking. Whatever sickness it was that caused her to tremble was worse than ever, and it seemed that both her arms and legs wanted to twist around instead of move straight.

The second pod let out Cousin Yulia. Like Sirah, she also had a large pack slung across her back and another rucksack that was so heavy she held onto it with both hands. After a wait of several seconds, Cousin Haw appeared with his big arms holding a large box that made even Haw struggle under its weight.

Auntie Talla led the group across the path to where Denny was standing. "Are we ready?"

"Kettle isn't out yet," said Denny, "but he should be soon. Why did you bring so much stuff? I thought we agreed that we were going to leave all our things behind?"

The low suns sent purple shadows chasing across Auntie Talla's face. "This shuttle of yours, how long does it take to get to another world?"

Denny thought about it. There was signboards inside the spaceport that told about arrival and departures of shuttles, but he couldn't remember any of them actually telling how long the trips would be. "I don't know," he admitted.

"And how much food is on each shuttle–food that humans can eat?"

"I don't..."

"What about water? Do they have water?"

Denny slumped. "I don't know."

Auntie Talla held out one of the sacks she was carrying. "Here. Take this. You'll be happy we have it if it turns out the shuttle only serves up food fit for skynx."

The moisture-clouded door of the port hissed open and Kettle stepped out. Even from a distance Denny could see that Kettle was nervous, and as he hurried over to them, Denny could see that he was actually sweating.

"Is this everybody?" asked Kettle.

"Everybody that's coming," said Denny.

Disappointment flashed over Kettle's face, but after a moment he went on. "We need to go fast. All the dasiks are down at loading area five. I'm supposed to be there too, helping to load a shuttle for the chugs. But there's another shuttle waiting at the very first area–loading area one. It's not supposed to fly until Dimsday, but when we get inside, that's where we're going."

"What if the dasiks see us?" asked Yulia.

"If they do..." Kettle shrugged. "I don't know. Come on. Let's just hurry."

They went up the ramp with Kettle in the lead. Despite the urgency, there was only so fast they could move, laden down with bags and boxes of food. Even if they hadn't been carrying a thing, Auntie Flash was still having trouble moving at more than a slow walk.

"It stinks in here," Cousin Haw loudly as they entered the port.

"It always does," said Kettle. "You kind of get used to it."

They went up the ramp inside the door. Kettle stood beside his mother, letting Auntie Flash lean on him as they moved toward the first area. Despite his size, Haw staggered along under the weight of the box, leaning back and holding it against his chest. Denny wondered just how many mummions and poppers, and how many blocks of chez, Auntie Talla had packed inside.

To Denny it seemed as if the spaceport had stretched out. The distance from the door to the first loading area wasn't a few dozen steps, it was more like a few thousand, and during every one of them he expected a dasik to appear, its long fingers clutching a weapon. The curve of the hall inside the port was great enough that they couldn't see past loading area three, but Denny thought he could spot shadows of motion around the curve and hear the dasiks at their work.

Kettle helped Auntie Flash to a space near the door. "We're going right through here," he said, speaking quietly. "When we get outside, go straight to the shuttle. The loading door is open, so we should be able to go right inside."

Everyone nodded. Kettle raised his hand and laid it against a pad beside the door. Nothing happened. He raised his hand, and then pressed it back again. The door remained closed.

"What's wrong?" asked Auntie Flash.

Kettle waved his hand at the plate a third time. "I don't know. It should open."

Denny took a few steps down the hall, craning his neck to be sure the dasiks weren't approaching. "Is there another way? Maybe if we go down to area three..."

"No. If we go that far, we'll be seen. Besides, there are walls outside between the landing areas."

Yulia stepped up beside Kettle. "This is the lock?"

Kettle nodded. His face was fixed in concentration as he slowly raised his hand to it again. "It opens when I put my palm to it. Or when the dasiks touch it with their claws."

"Only not this time." Yulia leaned in closer. She dropped the rucksack she was carrying, then put a finger on the glass next to the pad, tracing an almost invisible line beneath the surface. "I think I see," she said. Everyone tried to lean in closer as Yulia followed the line up and away.

"What did you find?" asked Denny.

Yulia looked around at Kettle. "Have you ever tried to get to a shuttle on a day it wasn't scheduled before?"

"Sure," said Kettle. Then his expression changed. "I mean...I think so. Except, well, maybe no." He shrugged. "I guess I never had a reason to try."

"Right." Yulia nodded. She looked around at them all. "I think this pad is connected to some kind of central control. Probably some kind of maton. It not only knows who is supposed to be here, it knows which areas are active."

"So we can't get in?" said Auntie Talla.

"No. Except." Yulia ran one hand through the tangled mass of her curls. "I think there might be a way." She reached into the pocket of her oversized jacket.

Before Yulia even had her hand free of her pocket, Denny realized what she was doing. He dashed toward her. "No, Yulia. You can't."

Yulia's hand reappeared. In it was the cloth-wrapped form of the silver maton. "Athena talked to other matons before. She can probably talk to this one, too."

Denny reached out toward her, but hesitated. "You can't."

Sirah appeared at his elbow. "Yulia, please don't. You saw what it did to Poppa Jam."

For a moment, Yulia only stared at the object in her hand. Slowly, she nodded. "You're right. It is dangerous."

Denny started to relax. "If we leave now—"

Before he could finish the sentence, Yulia ripped off the cloth covering and took a firm hold on the silver ball. For one terrible second, her body convulsed. Her chin went up, and the muscles of her neck and face grew so tight that she bared her teeth in a horrible grin of pain. Then Yulia relaxed.

"Yulia?"

"It's okay," she said. "I'm okay."

It was clear that Athena was once again visible to Yulia, as she quickly began explaining the situation and asked the woman from the maton if she could open the door. "Yes, right now." Yulia looked around, taking her eyes from the place in space where Athena was standing. "She's talking to the port maton. It should take just a second."

No sooner has she said this, than a tone sounded from the lock plate. The door to loading area one slid open.

"Everyone out," said Kettle. "Hurry."

Denny grabbed the bag that Yulia had been carrying and followed Kettle and Auntie Flash through the door. Outside, the tarmac of the shuttle area was crisscrossed with shadows, but as Kettle had said, the massive form of the shuttle itself was directly in front of the door. He could have run faster, but with Auntie Flash at the front of the line and Cousin Haw weighted with a huge box at the other end, it seemed to take the little line of humans a good slice of forever just to cross the few dozen steps to the bottom of the shuttle.

The biting smell of ammonia followed them through the door, but there was another, even stronger smell here. A heavy, burnt smell tinged with ozone. The tarmac crunched slightly with every footstep, as if the whole place had been baked hard as a cracker. Even just walking across the space seemed to release more of that burnt smell.

When Denny finally stumbled up the bronze metal of the shuttle ramp, he felt both relief and awe. The machine was as large as the one he had helped Kettle load before. The room at the base of the shuttle was easily as large as the gather room where Auntie Talla held Restaurant, and the ceiling was twice as high. At the moment, all that space was empty. When they dropped their few bags and boxes into the space, it seemed like a few crumbs in a huge empty closet.

Denny tossed the bag he was carrying in with the rest and turned around. Down the ramp, he could see back across the tarmac to the door of the port. There was still no sign of the dasiks, but he couldn't imagine that would last much longer. If nothing else, the dasiks were sure to notice that Kettle hadn't returned. "Close the ramp."

"Right." Kettle walked over to the side of the big space. On the wall of the empty storage bay was a group of panels, similar to the one that Kettle had touched when trying to open the door. But this time, he hadn't even raised his hand before a deep frown cross his face. "This isn't the way it's supposed to be."

"What's wrong?"

"I..." He stopped, turned around, and waved to Yulia. "Over here," he called.

Yulia seemed to be slow as she approached them, moving as if she was half asleep. Denny saw that the maton was still in her hand. Before Kettle could even explain the problem, she looked at them and said, "It's broken."

"Fix it," said Denny. "Like you did the door."

Yulia was silent for a moment, then she shook her head. "It's not like that," she said. "This shuttle came in early because it has problems. Athena says it's scheduled to be serviced later today, and it can't work right now. There's no power. None at all."

Kettle looked as if he'd been kicked. "I didn't know," he said. He turned around until he was facing his mother. "I didn't know," he repeated.

"Of...course...you didn't," said Auntie Flash.

Denny went to the top of the ramp and looked around. As Kettle had said, there were walls all around the space where the shuttle was sitting. There were gates in the walls, but they were all closed. "What do we do now?"

"We leave," said Auntie Talla. "It was a good try, but it didn't work. We leave."

Cousin Haw started to pick up the heavy box, but Auntie Talla waved him off. "Leave it. Let's just go."

Denny clenched his fists in frustration. He knew Talla was right. If the shuttle didn't work, they weren't likely to fix it, and if they stayed too long, the dasiks would come. But it seemed wrong. Badly wrong. Getting away from the planet was their only chance.

Sirah came up beside him. "Denny? What are we..."

Before she could finish, an alarm began to sound.

31

For a time that seemed like both an instant and an eternity, Denny was in compete panic. He wanted to run for the door. He wanted to hide among the bags. He wanted to pound on the controls of the shuttle until the huge machine decided it wasn't broken after all. It wasn't until Sirah grabbed his arm that he came back to himself and began to think.

"Can we still go back into the port?" Sirah asked above the rising and falling sound of the alarm.

"I think... No." Denny took a few steps down the ramp and quickly scanned the fences. On one side, the side behind the shuttle, he saw that there was one gate set back from the wall, surrounded by short walls on each side. "Kettle," he called. "Where does that gate go?"

Kettle turned to look where Denny was pointing. "Outside."

"Can you open it?

A quick shake of the head. "No."

"Yulia." Denny ran back to where the girl was standing against the wall, took her by the hand and led her to the bottom of the ramp. Her face was drawn, and she seemed to sway on her feet, but her right hand was still clutching firmly to the silver ball.

Before he could say more, Auntie Talla saw what he was doing. "Sirah," she said. "Get over to that gate. Haw, go with her." She looked at Denny. "Do you have her?"

Denny nodded. With Denny on one arm and Kettle on the other side, they guided Yulia over to the walled gate.

"Can Athena open it?" Denny asked.

There was a terrible moment in which Yulia gave no answer, then at last her face relaxed. "She can, but it's going to take a second. She's negotiating with the base maton."

It took more than a second. It took thirty seconds. A minute. "Yulia..."

She held up her left hand. "Athena's working on it. Almost there."

Then two things happened at once. The lock on the gate made a metallic tonk, and the gate began to slowly slide open. In the same moment, there was a tone behind them, a tone that Denny recognized as the door from the loading area being opened. He turned, trying to make sure that everyone was hidden from view behind the short walls that flanked the gate to the outside... and saw Auntie Flash.

Auntie Flash was walking–slowly, but with steadier steps than Denny had seen her make in months–straight toward the opening door. She was already more than a dozen steps away, halfway across the space from the shuttle to the spaceport. A pair of dasiks appeared. They were not merely touching the stunstiks, they were carrying them raised in long-fingered hands. The blue-gray metal of the stiks flashed in the air. The dasiks came toward her at a run, their long legs eating up the space between them in just a few strides.

There was a sound from Denny's left. Not a word, just a kind of "mumph." He turned his head, and saw that Kettle was standing there. Or not standing. Kettle was actually leaning forward, his feet scuffling against the ground. Holding him was Cousin Haw. One of Haw's thick arms was clamped across Kettle's chest. Haw's other hand was pressed hard against Cousin Kettle's mouth. Above Haw's blunt fingers, Kettle's eyes were full of shock and desperation.

"You caught me," said Auntie Flash loudly. Like her steps, her voice was surprisingly steady. "I just wanted to see a shuttle before I was consigned."

The dasiks closed on her in a scramble of movement. They didn't press any buttons. They didn't say anything. The pair of stunstiks came down on Auntie Flash with such force that Denny could hear the solid thunk from across the tarmac. Could feel it in his stomach. The blows didn't so much knock Auntie Flash from her feet as drive her into the scorched ground. She crumpled straight down on herself, her legs folding beneath her. Her head and shoulders twisted around at an angle to the rest of her, as if, in the middle of falling, she had tried to turn back for a final glimpse of the others. Of Kettle.

A hand took Denny by the arm. "Let's go," said Sirah in an urgent whisper.

Denny turned and saw that the door was open. Cousin Haw had already pulled a struggling Kettle through the opening. Yulia was through, though she looked as if she was about to fall. Auntie Talla was holding Yulia by one arm, guiding her. The door began to close. Denny followed Sirah through the gap before it could disappear. He turned his head at the last moment.

Out on the tarmac, the dasiks were carrying Auntie Flash away.

32

As soon as Cousin Haw put him down, Kettle started running. It took both Denny and Sirah to tackle Kettle long enough for Haw to grab him again.

"I have to get in there," said Kettle. "I can talk to them. They know me."

"They know you," said Auntie Talla. "And if you go back in there, you won't come out. They have to know that you're the one who let your mother in. They're probably looking for you right now."

Kettle's face fell in on itself in a way that reminded Denny of the way Auntie Flash had fallen in front of the dasiks. With Haw's hand still on his shoulder, Kettle walked with the rest of them down to the ground transport.

Denny wished that there was some other way to get away from the spaceport. They could walk—it was a long trip back to the quarter, though he'd done it several times—but seven humans...no, six. Now they were six. Six humans walking together down any street in Jukal Plex would attract a lot of attention. A lot of anger from cithians. But transport pods seemed a ridiculous way to make an escape. To go only a hundred steps away from the front of the building they'd just left, then queue up politely, waiting for the pods to arrive. It was like part of an awful joke. If the dasiks realized that Auntie Flash wasn't alone–and they had to, had to be looking for Cousin Kettle at least–then all they had to do was step outside to find them.

Meanwhile, Kettle was still arguing that he needed to go back in, while both Auntie Talla and Sirah tried to convince him that the dasiks would bring his mother back to the quarter. Denny didn't think anyone else had seen the way the dasiks struck Auntie Flash. He wasn't sure that they were going to take her anywhere at all.

A ground transport appeared in the distance and started down the last sweeping curve to the port. Every second of its approach increased the tension in Denny's mind. Not only did he expect the dasiks to come charging toward them out of the port, he was suddenly convinced that the transport was going to arrive filled with cithians. He could already see them waving their forelimbs. Hear the rapid-fire trill of clangers signaling anger.

The transport pulled up to the stop, the doors of the two pods opened. Empty. A moment later everyone was aboard, Cousin Haw still dragging a struggling Kettle, and the transport was gliding smoothly away, back toward the heart of the plex. Without all the bags of supplies they had carried out to the port–and of course, without Auntie Flash–they all fit into a single pod. There was a strange silence in the pod. Auntie Talla spoke softly to Kettle, who said nothing in reply. Denny was relieved to see that Yulia had finally released her hold on the maton, but the effect of using the device again had left her looking ashen, like she had been sick for a week.

Denny pressed his face up against the clear side of the pod and watched the plex slide past. He had made this trip many times, but this was probably the last. Everything was the last. He'd made his last trip to the Porium. He'd eaten his last Restaurant. Made his last trip to the port. He'd seen Loma for the last time. Seen Poppa Jam for the last time. And maybe seen Auntie Flash for the last time.

He stared out across Jukal Plex, with its circles of supply domes, sleeping stadiums, and work blocks. On the far side of the plex, the tall white spike of the Cataclysm cast twin shadows across the nearest buildings. The low blue sun spread its shadows so far that for a moment, the train passed through that near darkness. Maybe this would also be the last time Denny saw the plex. Or anything.

The ground transport reached the stop nearest the human quarter and they all filed off. Now even Kettle seemed quiet. There was no longer a need for Haw to hold onto him, but Kettle walked along with his shoulders hunched and an expression on his face that seemed to be half sorrow, half rage. Denny couldn't blame him. He stared down at the worn toes of his shoes. They'd had just one chance to get away, and instead they had lost one of their own. Or maybe there had never been a chance at all.

Denny suddenly bumped into someone. He looked up and saw Sirah looking away from him, down the street. "What's wrong?" he asked. It seemed like a stupid question. *Everything* was wrong.

"Look," replied Sirah. She raised her head, pointing with her chin past the old gate markers into the quarter. Between the compartment buildings and the low buildings of the stores, a dozen cithians were in motion. There were dasiks, too. These dasiks weren't carrying stunstiks. They were holding... something else. None of the cithians or dasiks in the quarter seemed to have spotted the group of humans standing at the gates, but that was surely a matter of seconds.

"Over here," Denny said. "Hurry."

He led them through the broken side door into one of the buildings just on the other side of the gate. It was the same building where Denny had put on the moltling costume. That had been only four days before, though it seemed like years. The chemical smell in the building seemed to be stronger than Denny remembered it. When everyone was inside, he closed the door.

"What are they doing here?" asked Sirah. Her voice was barely a whisper. "Is it because we were at the spaceport? Do they know we were all there?"

"Maybe," said Auntie Talla, also speaking softly, though the cithians were a hundred steps away. "Or maybe they are here because it's their day to be here. Maybe this is the day we are all to be consigned."

Whatever the reason, no one seemed anxious to try and talk with the cithians. They milled around the front room of the building, past the old benches and tables. There was only a single small window in the building that faced back into the quarter. Haw and Kettle stood beside it, staring back down the cracked pavement of the street.

"I don't see–" started Kettle. "No. There's a dasik. Two more. They're carrying something." He watched a few seconds more, then turned away and slumped against the wall.

"What?" asked Sirah. "What is it?"

Kettle looked down at the floor. "Poppa Gow's chair."

After that, Cousin Haw kept up the watch, but the rest of them spread out around the room. Yulia, who had said little since leaving the port, rested on one of the benches with her back against the wall. As far as Denny could tell, she was asleep. Sirah sat down beside her, folding her arms on a table and resting her head. The heavy braid of her hair had pulled loose from her head-cloth, and it brushed a path through thick dust. Denny found that, tired as he was, he could not sit still. He paced around the room, his hands opening and closing. There had to be something. There had to be something.

Auntie Talla simply stood in the center of the room, stiffly upright, with her arms folded across her chest. Her head turned slightly to follow Denny. "What now?"

"I don't know." Denny stopped in his tracks and looked at her. "Thank you," he said.

"For what?"

"For believing me. For listening to me. For fixing such good things to eat at Restaurant and never making me pay more than I had."

A quick bark of laughter escaped Auntie Talla. "That seems like a small thing to think about now."

"Believe me," said Denny. "It isn't. It never was to me."

The hard expression on Auntie Talla's face faltered. She turned away from him and put her hands to her face. Her back shook softly.

Denny wandered out of the big room into the long room with the stains on the wall. There were no windows here. Just the low benches against one wall and the row of pipes and nozzles. He was about to walk back to the other room when he saw something on the floor. At first he thought it was just a rag, maybe something left over from assembling his moltling disguise. But when he stepped closer, he saw a stripe of color, a band of yellow barely visible in the faint skimsday light that filtered in from the other room.

He reached down to pick it up and found that the cloth was actually wrapped around something else, something solid and dense. Denny carefully unfolded the layers and found that what was inside was a book. Not a picture book, but a word book. A book like the one that Loma had given him.

It was a slim volume, with only a single word for a title. It was one of those words that Denny didn't know, but he knew the book. He knew it was one of Loma's. She had been here sometime in the last few days.

Denny opened the cover of the book. He had only read one book before, and he hadn't even really read that one. Just picked at it, reading the words he could read, trying to make some sense of the story from what little he could make out. This book was much harder in a way. There seemed to be so many words that he didn't know. From what he could tell, it was about some people, many people, who were being held prisoner by some other people. But the book was full of names for places and for things and for people that didn't mean anything to Denny. In the middle of one page, a line had been drawn under a single sentence. Denny guessed it was Loma who had drawn the line. Or maybe someone who had owned the book before Loma. Even in this one line, he couldn't make out all the words. But he could make out enough.

To forget the dead would be...killing them a second time.

33

He walked back into the other room and went straight to Yulia. He thought she was asleep, but as Denny got closer, her eyes opened.

"I want to talk to her," he said.

Yulia didn't ask who Denny meant. She only tugged open the pocket of her big jacket and stretched it out toward Denny. Inside, he could see the glimmer of metal.

Sirah raised her head from the table. "No. Denny, don't."

Denny reached into the pocket and took the maton firmly in hand. The pain ripped through him. It seemed worse than before, but then it was hard to remember pain. It was just...pain.

Athena was there. Only she was no longer the stone woman Denny had met in the storage dome. She was one of them. Athena had Yulia's weight of heavy dark curls. She had bare arms that looked both slender and strong, like Sirah's. She had deep brown eyes that Denny didn't recognize, but which she had surely stolen from some other human. Even her clothes looked like theirs— raggedy, old, and bleached down to just the ghost of colors.

Denny wasn't fooled. No matter what she looked like, Athena wasn't really a human. She was a thing. A machine. "Tell me why," he said to her.

Athena cocked her head to the side. That faint smile was on her lips again. "Why?"

"Tell me why they hate us so much." He shook his fist toward the small window at the far end of the room. "Tell me why they kill us."

Athena nodded. "I have pertinent information regarding that question," she said. A light appeared in the middle of the room.

Auntie Talla whipped around. "What's that?"

Sirah scrambled to her feet as the light began to form shapes. "Denny? Are you doing that?"

"She's doing it," he said. He turned to Athena. "I thought you could only show things to the person holding the maton?"

"I am only visible to the user in interface," she said. "However, other materials are less limited."

The light in the middle of the room resolved into images. A voice began to speak.

34

TRANQUILITY

The planet Rask lies in a stable orbit around the gravitation center of the binary star system, Andersen-Ikirii 204. Rask is nearly tidally locked at a position near the white dwarf, though the actual position is offset slightly toward the gravitational center of the system. The result is that one side of the planet enjoys fairly equitable conditions, with the white dwarf star visible continuously for most of the central land mass. The opposite side of the planet is cold, and has very little plant life.

The species commonly referred to as cithian evolved 1.6 million years ago on the second largest of Rask's continents. Over the next million years, they reached all areas of the planet, survived a period of usually high stellar output, and successfully established communities on the colder, less habitable side of the planet as well as establishing large settlements on every part of the star-facing side of the planet.

A strongly structured civilization was established. Large scale architecture developed. A series of wars were fought, which led a gradual consolidation of the planetary government. Significant advancements were made in mathematics. Engineering. Logistics. For 348,000 years, cithians built on this foundation. They learned to predict the weather despite variations in their planet's path through the binary star system. They learned to make wheels. They learned to make both bronze and iron. They developed, and discarded, several philosophies about the nature of existence. They built an elaborate social system, a language rich in both syntax and symbol, and art forms that were both subtle and meaningful.

In the 186,542nd year since the cithians achieved a unified government, the leaders of the government were gathered at a place then called Palakajukal to evaluate the completion of a wide scale irrigation project which would reduce flooding and provide more reliable resources for agriculture. On the day now regarded as the first day of the first year on the cithian calendar, a light appeared in the sky. The light grew brighter until it rivaled the glow of the sun. Of both suns. Finally, the light came to hover over Palakajukal. With great peals of thunder that sent many cithians running in panic, the light descended. It was an alien starship.

The aliens within the starship came out to meet the cithian leaders, bringing with them the fundamentals of electricity, electronics, and the richness of information theory. They brought advanced optics, astronomy, and the history of the universe. They brought a deep understanding of biology, evolution, and a cure for many diseases. They brought the theory of gravitation, of relativity, of quantum states and multiverses. They brought the ability to harness fundamental forces, to transform the planet, and to sail among the stars.

The aliens onboard the ship came in a spirit of friendship. And generosity.

The cithians found that, while the alien technology was radically advanced compared to their own, it was nothing they could not learn with study. So they studied. They found that the alien art and the alien philosophies had aspects that they had never considered. They considered them. The many alien breakthroughs were puzzling when you didn't understand the basics, but if you applied yourself to a few fundamental points, they became obvious. The cithians applied themselves.

Within a generation, the cithians had incorporated almost all the knowledge that the aliens had brought them. And within a generation, almost nothing remained of the cithian civilization. The achievements of their greatest minds were revealed as primitive. The most important events of their past were cataloged and recorded in one, rather slim, volume. Their artworks were digitized. Their philosophies duly noted. The thoughts and lives and the stories that had sustained their people since the beginning, became quaint.

The aliens—the humans—who came in the starship and brought this change to the cithians, were part of a culture that was a bit less than 13,000 years old.

35

Denny watched the last images of the story Athena showed them fade into darkness. He had watched it three times, though holding onto the maton so long had made him ache with tiredness that went down to his bones. During the second showing, he had to sit down. During the third, Sirah put an arm around him to keep him from slumping over on the bench. Denny found it hard to stop even then. Long after the images had disappeared from the air, they were still playing in his mind. The long ramp descending. The humans in their bulky white suits coming down to greet the baffled cithians.

"We found them," said Sirah. Then again, her voice thick with sad wonder. "We found them."

On the other side of Denny, across from Sirah, sat Athena. She seemed to be watching the images along with everyone else, though her smile never faltered.

Denny turned toward her. His neck felt hot and stiff. "How did things go so wrong after that?" he asked the artificial woman. "How did Earth end up so polluted we could never go home?"

"It didn't," Athena said.

Denny felt like he should not be surprised. Everything he thought he knew about the past was turning out to be wrong. "Then, if we could get a shuttle, we could go to Earth?"

Athena nodded. "You could. However, Earth's biosphere was badly damaged by bombing in the thirteenth year of the war. Though recent records are not available to me, it is unlikely that current conditions on that planet are favorable for complex life."

"Earth...is dead?" It shouldn't hurt to lose a home he'd never visited, a planet he'd always thought was lost anyway. It hurt. "In a war?"

"The war to destroy Earth and all human colonies," said Athena. "I'm sorry. I do not have presentation materials on this subject."

Denny guessed that meant there would be no more moving pictures. Or at least, none about this war. He knew the word. There was war in some of his picture books, with missiles and bombs and rays of fire lashing out at evil space ships. "How could they? If the cithians were so far behind humans, how could they beat us?"

Athena stood and appeared to slowly pace around the room. It was a movement Denny had seen before. He wondered if it was built into the memory—designed to make her seem more like a real person. "They didn't," she said. "Not alone. It was a coalition of several races, working together, that was successful in defeating humanity."

Denny found that he was actually crying, And he found that he was right back to the question he had asked before. "But why? Why did they do it?"

"Because you were too quick," said Athena. "Because you were too unpredictable. Because you spread so far, so fast. Because you would not stop looking in the next system, and the next, to see what was there. Because you could not stop confusing kindness and interference. Because you always thought you were right." She stopped her pacing and turned to face him. "Because you destroyed them first, by trying to make them like you. And because you expected them to be grateful."

Denny let go of the maton, and Athena disappeared in a blink.

36

DIMSDAY

On Dimsday, Denny watched the world end. He woke suddenly up out of confused dreams. Dreams about his father and a great jagged sculpture that was as tall as a building. At the other end of the long room, Cousin Haw lay face down on a long bench, his heavy arms dragged on the floor, and grinding snores escaped his mouth as his thick body went up and down in time with his breathing. Cousin Kettle was nearby, sitting with his back to a corner and his arms around his knees. Yulia had taken her jacket off to act as a pillow. Auntie Talla had done the same with her cloak.

Sirah was awake. Denny slowly got to his feet and walked across the darkened room. It was Dimsday, and even the light of the tiny blue sun was blocked by neighboring buildings. The air inside the low building had cooled while they rested until it was more than a little chilly. The streets of the quarter were in all but complete darkness.

As Denny drew up beside her, Sirah turned to him. "Did you hear it?"

"Hear what?"

"That sound." Sirah shivered. "It was like... I think it was a person."

Together they stood by the small window. The street outside was empty. A block away, a small light glowed at the door of the compartment building where both Denny and Sirah lived. Had lived. High above the street, he saw lights in other windows, but no movement.

He was just about to say something more when he heard it–a high, thin noise that cut off abruptly. It might not have been a human at all, but Denny didn't think so. He thought it was Nonni Hacci. Or Auntie Fro. Or maybe Auntie Flash. He didn't know what was causing them to make that sound, but he knew it couldn't be good. "Earth," he said.

Sirah clutched his arm. "Careful," she whispered. "Don't wake Kettle." She touched the window. Circles of fog appeared around her fingertips. "I've been thinking about the the moving pictures you saw."

"I thought you saw them too."

"Not the ship," said Sirah. "The other pictures that you told me about. The ones you saw at Old Loma's."

Denny had to think for a moment. "About the disease."

"Yes," she said. "I think...I think that's what they did to us."

"I don't understand. What?"

"What they did with the disease," said Sirah. "The people who destroyed it kept some of it around, just in case it turned out it wasn't really gone."

"And when they thought that it was—"

"They got rid of the last bits." Sirah nodded. "That's what they did with us."

There was a motion behind them. Denny turned and saw Auntie Talla rising. She rubbed at her arms, then gathered up her cloak and pulled it around her. "Can you see anything?" she asked softly.

"No, but—"

"I know," she said. "I heard it." Shivering, she took a step closer to the window. "We can't stay here. We all needed a rest, but it's only luck that's kept them from finding us so far. Besides, we don't have any food. We have to go."

Denny wished he had an answer. "Where can we go?"

"I don't know," said Talla. "We have to find somewhere they won't think of. Somewhere we can take care of ourselves."

"Where?"

Talla's face was fixed in the same look of determination that Denny had seen on a hundred nights when she had found a way to feed everyone in the quarter. A way to hold them together. "I don't know," she said. "We have to find somewhere."

"I know where," said a voice from across the room. Yulia raised up off her bench, stretching as she unfolded her jacket and slipped it back on. "Didn't you see it?"

"See what?" asked Denny.

"The place. Where we should go." Yulia looked around the room. "Where's the maton?"

Denny pointed to where the silver ball had rolled when he had dropped it. "Do you think you should be touching it? You used it a long time yesterday."

"No longer than you." Yulia reached under the bench and wrapped her hand around the maton. Denny saw her neck snap back and her body tremble as the pain ran through her. She licked her lips. "Athena, I need to see the moving pictures you were showing before." The images began to hover in the middle of the room, showing the blue-gray sphere of a planet floating in space. "Not from the beginning. Go to the part where the ship lands."

The image showed a cithian complex. It was tiny compared to the current city, and the buildings were composed of stone and wood. As the brilliant torch of the approaching ship came down from above, Denny could even make out the tiny figures of cithians scurrying away from the point of landing. The image gradually closed in on the base of the starship as it came to rest on a lightning-scarred plane outside the cithian town.

"There," said Yulia. "Athena, stop it there." She walked toward the floating image. "Do you see?"

Denny frowned at the shapes. He could see the shadows from the cithian buildings, the frozen lightning at the ship's base, and the gleaming lower third of the ship itself, but he didn't know what Yulia was talking about.

"There," she said, running her finger through the image of the ship. "Right there." She looked at them all. "Don't you recognize it? The human ship? It's the Cataclysm."

37

They filed out of the building an hour later. Because it was Dimsday, not only the quarter but all of Jukal seemed to be deserted. Most of the cithians in the plex would be in the sleeping stadiums, resting until the next day.

Cousin Kettle argued that they should go into the quarter. They could get food. Find other things they would need. It took Auntie Talla to talk him out of it. "Your mother did what she did for your sake," she said. "Don't throw it away."

They shuffled out of the building, staying close to the grimy walls. There was no motion in the quarter. No motion ahead of them. There were a pair of road ferries near the end of the small road leading into the quarter, but there were no cithians or dasiks in sight. It seemed just possible that they could take a transport all the way around the city, to where the great bulk of the Cataclysm waited.

There was a small shelter at the stop. They crowded under and around it as Auntie Talla pressed the button to summon the transport. "When it gets here, I'll set it to go around the outside of the plex, past the market. That way we'll avoid the heart of the cithian areas." It seemed like a good idea.

As they waited, clouds began to pile up in the west, making the dark day even darker. It rarely rained in Jukal, but when it did water often came in great, greasy downpours. Within a few minutes, the first heavy drops began to fall, splashing down like cups emptied overhead.

Kettle leaned out into the gathering storm and turned toward the heart of the plex. "Where are the pods?" he said. "They should have been here by now."

Auntie Talla, one of the few humans who regularly traveled outside the quarter, quickly agreed. "You're right. Especially on Dimsday."

Denny looked around. Something was wrong. Very wrong. He thought he heard a sound in the distance, a noise that was like a whole mass of cithians clanging an alarm against their shells. "They're coming," he said. "They know we're here." He stepped away from the shelter. Fat drops of rain splashed over his head and shoulders. The air rumbled with distant thunder, but over that sound he could still hear the alarm. It was coming closer.

"Come on!" he shouted, then he began to run back toward the quarter.

"Where are you going?" Sirah called after him.

"The ferries!"

Denny reached the first road ferry. The control to open it was in the same place as the one he had ridden in with the skynx, and one touch was enough to flip back the curved top. The rain made popping sounds as it struck the seats.

The other humans arrived a second later. "Do you know how to make this move?" asked Talla.

"I think so. Get in."

The ferry was larger than most, big enough to hold two adult cithians comfortably, but fitting six humans inside was still difficult. Denny found himself sharing the front seat with Kettle in the middle and Sirah on the other side. Talla and Yulia squeezed into the back with Cousin Haw. When everyone was in, Denny touched the entry panel again and the top swung back into position. Now the rain drummed on the top of the ferry. The approaching alarm was much louder, and from close at hand Denny could hear the voices of cithians.

He looked across the front of the ferry. There were two short rods at each side of the space, and a flat pad in the center. Denny stretched to touch the pad. Nothing happened. "Yulia!"

"Already doing it," she said from the back. The whole ferry shook as Yulia jerked from touching the maton. "Athena, get us going," she said. Then after a moment. "The Cataclysm." The ferry started to move.

Denny craned his neck. He could see figures coming toward them from out of the quarter, and from the direction of the nearest sleeping dome, but the ferry was rapidly picking up speed. In a few seconds, the entrance to the quarter was left behind, invisible through the increasing rain. Denny drew in a deep breath and let it out slowly. In a road ferry it should take only a few minutes to get to the huge spaceship.

The ferry rounded the curve past the transport stop. It turned left at the next inbound spoke, then turned right again at the first opportunity. "Are you sure we're going the right way?"

Yulia nodded. "Athena says she's picking the fastest way. We should be there …uh oh." The sound of the ferry changed and they glided to a stop in the rain.

"What's wrong?" asked Sirah.

Yulia held up a hand for silence. "Yes… Yes… There has to be something."

Denny wondered where in the crowded ferry Yulia was seeing Athena. "What's wrong?"

"It's the maton that runs the traffic for the plex. It's shut down the ferry. Athena is trying to get it running again."

Denny twisted round in his seat. There were shapes back there in the rain. Shapes that were coming fast. He looked back at the front of the ferry. "Can she turn it off?"

"Turn off the ferry?"

"Turn off the maton's control. Make the ferry drive on its own." He pushed the short bar on his side of the car back and forth. "I mean, make it so we can make the ferry go."

"I don't... okay. Yes," said Yulia. "She can do that."

Talla spoke up from the rear. "Then do it now. There's another ferry just a block away, and it's coming toward us."

"Done," said Yulia. "Go!"

Denny bit his lip and reached for the bar in front of him. Kettle reached for it at the same time. The bar moved with surprising ease, and together they slammed it hard forward. The ferry spun sickeningly around quickly to the right. In moments they were facing completely back the way they had come–directly at the approaching ferry. Denny tried pulling on the bar. Kettle was still pushing.

"Let go!"

Kettle let go. The ferry spun back to its original position, but didn't move forward.

"Let me try the other one." Sirah grabbed for the bar on her side and pushed. The ferry spun left.

A dark shape loomed up behind them. The other ferry was right next to them. From the corner of his eye Denny saw the shape of a dasik no more than a step away.

"Keep pushing!" He shoved at his bar again. With both bars shoved forward the ferry lurched ahead. As Denny and Sirah struggled with the controls, the ferry gathered speed as it swerved left, right, left again. The ferry bounced up from the street, hurtled over the sidewalk, brushed against the side of a building, and banked back into the street. There was a heavy thud and a bump as the ferry rolled over something. Lightning cracked directly overhead, and for a moment the street ahead was lit in stark light, then the light was gone and the ferry plunged ahead in darkness.

"What are you doing?" Talla shouted from the rear seat.

"It's harder than it looks," said Denny.

"Slow down, or we're not going to need the cithians to kill us."

"Left!" Yulia shouted suddenly from the back seat. "Turn left,"

Denny, still dazzled by the lightning, couldn't see the road, or the buildings or anything. He pressed forward, then thought again and pulled back. He couldn't see what Sirah did on her controls, but suddenly the ferry spun in place so quickly that Denny's head cracked against the side. He saw shadows through the glass beside his face, enough to see that they were passing close to a sleeping stadium. Then they were moving forward again, speeding not across a street, but in the rough ground between the stadium and a storage dome. A work block loomed up on the left, and Denny pressed forward just in time to avoid its mass. Another storage dome appeared on the right. Denny tugged back on the stick. The right side of the ferry actually swerved part way up the wall of the dome before crashing back to the ground. Denny glanced over just long enough to see Sirah furiously working the bar on her side back and forth. And to see that Kettle was looking sort of green.

"Which way?" Sirah called.

"No idea," said Denny.

"Right," said Yulia. "Right....now. Turn right now!"

Denny shoved forward. Sirah pulled back. The ferry pivoted in a moment. When they straightened, Denny was surprised to see that they were actually hurtling straight down the center of a rain-slick street. The ferry was moving fast, much faster than he had ever seen one move when he was out in the plex. Buildings whipped by on both left and right. Another flash of lightning showed a single cithian traveling along the wet sidewalk. "Which way now?"

"This way," said Yulia. "Just keep going."

Denny wanted to turn his head to see how close the other ferry was to them, but he didn't dare look away from the road. In the next flash of lightning, he saw something ahead of them. Something that loomed pale and huge across the entire road.

"Stop," said Yulia.

Sirah responded right away. Denny a moment later. It was enough of a difference to launch the ferry hard to the right. It bounded up a slope, smashed through a tall fence, rolled up onto one side, came down again, and spun to a halt against a wall of pale metal.

"We're here," said Yulia.

Denny slapped at the plate beside him and the top of the ferry opened. Lightning still flickered above them and the ground vibrated with thunder, but the rain had slowed to a few widely spaced drops. Denny climbed weakly out of the ferry. Looking back, he saw nothing in the street behind them but bits of broken stone and a metal panel knocked loose from the side of the ferry.

Kettle and Sirah came out after him. Both of them seemed to be okay. From the back seat, Yulia and Talla climbed out quickly, but Cousin Haw took several seconds to appear. Even in the poor light, Denny could see that the big man was shaking.

"Did we get away from the other ferry?" asked Denny.

"Ten minutes ago," said Auntie Talla. "I don't think they thought about driving on things that weren't streets."

"How far are we from the Cataclysm?"

"What do you mean?" asked Yulia. She put a hand on the wall of metal near the nose of the ferry. "This is it."

38

Denny stared in surprise. He'd seen the Cataclysm from across the city all his life, but he'd never appreciated how enormous it really was. The side of the thing was so large that from close up it was hard to tell it was even curved. Overhead it rose into the darkness, the top actually lost in clouds. The sheer size made Denny feel like coming here had been a mistake. The idea that they might actually move something so enormous was ridiculous.

"Which way do we go?" asked Sirah.

Yulia was still clutching the maton. She waved it to Denny's right. "This way."

The ground around the gigantic ship turned out to be actual ground. Soaked through by the heavy rain, it was spongy and slick underfoot. Denny slipped and staggered forward, resting one hand on the side of the ship for support.

"Wait," Talla's voice said from behind him.

Denny turned to see that Talla was holding something. It took him a moment to realize the something was Yulia. She was limp in Talla's arms, her head tilted forward and her curls dripping from the rain. Denny knelt down beside her, his knee sinking into the soggy ground. "Yulia. You have to put it down now."

She shook her head weakly. "Can't. We need her."

"We need you," said Talla.

Yulia raised herself slowly. "I'm okay. Let's just keep moving."

They started forward again. There was a small rise in the ground, but getting over it seemed to Denny like climbing a mountain. Sirah was right behind him. Kettle had moved back to help Talla with Yulia. Haw was far back, his feet sinking deep into the mud at every step.

Denny slipped, fell and slid down the slope on the other side. Another crack of lightning, and in the rumble that followed he made out a flat space ahead covered in plates of what seemed to be stone. There was a gap in the wall of the ship on the left. Some kind of opening. And there was something in the center of the stone plates. He took another step, then froze. It was a cithian. A cithian and...a human? The light flickered again. The way it glinted off the figures ahead let Denny know what he was actually seeing.

He came forward, his muddy shoes leaving streaks on the wet stones. The two shapes ahead of him came clearer at every step. It was a human. A human made of metal. A statue of a human, like the ones that his father had made, only this statue wasn't just as big as a person, it was bigger. The human in the statue was a giant, two heads taller than any person Denny had ever seen. He was wearing a suit with funny creases at elbow and knee. His face was set in an expression that Denny could not quite read. Happy. No, not happy. Something more than that.

The metal man held out one gloved hand to the figure in front of him. That figure was a cithian, taller even than the man, with the deep notches and groves along its metal shell that showed it was a leader among leaders. The cithian held out a mid-limb to the man. The man's fingers and the cithian's spiky manipulators were just touching.

Denny realized after a moment that Sirah had joined him. She trailed her hand across the metal back of the man. "A wonder who he was," she said.

Talla and Kettle struggled down the hill, holding Yulia between them.

"Earth," Kettle said softly.

Denny circled the two figures. There was something set into the stones beside them. It was a large yellowish metal sign, with words raised up in letters the size of Denny's hand. Despite the size of the words, the darkness made it hard to make out what it said. He had to wait till the next flicker from above before the first part was clear.

HERE HUMANS FROM EARTH... read the top of the sign. Another quick bolt of lightning. "...FIRST SET FOOT..."

Then lights were shining in Denny's face. Not the quick stab of lightning, but light that was steady and bright and coming from all sides. He raised his face to see three dasiks standing around the stone area with bright lights in one hand and stunstiks in the other. From the shadows Overcontroller Hiser appeared.

"Stop where you are." The cithian raised a forelimb, showing a blunt gun with a wide black barrel. "Your escape is over."

39

TOLLSDAY

On Tollsday, Denny surrendered. The clouds moved aside long enough to reveal a faint red glow in the sky that marked the start of Tollsday. Around them, the plex would be waking from its Dimsday sleep. The market would be opening. The streets would soon fill with cithians on their way to work.

In the increased light, Denny could see the tall fence that separated the base of the human starship from the buildings around it. It was tall enough that even a cithian wouldn't have been able to see over the top. Denny realized that it might not be just the humans who didn't understand the truth. How many generations of cithians had grown up thinking they had rescued the poor, helpless humans? How many of them knew what had really happened?

In the little stone square, everyone seemed to be frozen. Sirah leaned back against the tall statue of a human. Kettle stood protectively next to Yulia, one arm around her back. The silver orb was still in Yulia's hand, but her head was down, her face hidden. Auntie Talla stood in the center of the space. Her long cloak was wet and streaked with mud at the bottom, but her arms were folded over her chest. Her chin high. Behind them all the door into the ship was a circle of darkness—a mystery they would never reach.

From behind the bulk of the Overcontroller, a new figure appeared. Denny thought he was too tired to be surprised by anything, but he jumped to see that it was the old chug, the same chug who he had seen at the spaceport. The chug who had put the memory cube into his box.

The chug moved around to stand beside the Overcontroller. "I said I wanted to see a human thing," he said in his whispery voice, "and now I have." A dozen eyes, brown, blue, and orange, pivoted toward Denny. "I gave the least of you the tiniest chance, I dropped a bit of debris into the box of a beggar, and now here you are."

The chug glided toward Denny, its hidden limbs clicking softly. "That's a human thing. Curiosity. Restlessness. Jump, jump, jump. That is what you do."

It paused near the edge of the sign. Denny looked down, reading the golden words at the chug's feet. "We came in peace," he said.

"Peace." It was dangerous to read expression into the voices of other races, but there was little doubt the chug viewed the word as poison. "For half a million years, my people lived in the same way. In fullness and contentment. Then humans came, and in a single generation we wanted more. Progress. Change. Hope." He said the last three words with the same venom he had used for the word "Peace."

"So you killed us," said Talla.

The chug raised a quartet of eyes to look her way. "Not all of you, though that was not my choice." The eyes pointing toward Denny and Talla settled back into the mass, and a new cluster of blue and orange directed their focus toward the Overcontroller. "Your people are the ones who insisted on keeping these humans alive for so long. Will you at last acknowledge that they are too dangerous to allow even the slightest trace to survive?"

Hiser Grismalamacata Omicradiscrad, Overcontroller Human Assistance Authority, seemed to have a hard time answering this question. His jaws made a series of clicks, and his clangers thumped softly against his shell, once, then a second time. "I have...delayed this moment for many years," he said. He raised the big gun in his forelimb and pointed it toward Denny. "But this—"

Whatever he was going to say next, he didn't get the chance to finish. A red-black shape ran into the square so quickly that it was only after the Overcontroller was on the ground that Denny realized it was the slender, sharp form of Omi. The young cithian caught the heavy gun with one mid-limb and sent it flipping away. "Run, Denny," he said. "Quick."

Omi threw out a quick forelimb blow that grazed the chug, and a second blow just missed striking the chug in the middle of its curtain of eyes. The chug ran away with surprising speed.

The two dasiks standing behind Omi seemed frozen at first, but then they rushed in, stunstiks swinging. Denny turned to shout something to the others. He was turned just the right way to see another of the dasiks suddenly snap its long head back at the end of its long neck, and crumple to the muddy ground. Cousin Haw stepped out from behind the fallen dasik, his big fists raised.

"Get in the ship," shouted Talla. "Everyone."

Kettle dragged Yulia through the dark opening. Sirah hesitated at the entrance. "Come on!" she called to Denny.

Haw stepped over the fallen dasik and struggled down the last of the slope into the square. His boots were so caked with mud that it looked as if each leg was carrying a good portion of the hill. With a quick glance toward the place where Omi was struggling with the dasiks, Haw started for the opening.

Omi was lashing out with the sharp edges of his heavy forelimbs, but the armored skin of the dasiks turned back his blows. One of them reached in quickly, striking Omi with a stunstik. Both Omi's legs on that side collapsed.

The cithian tipped over, and fell to the side, but he kept fighting, striking out with both his forelimbs and his hindlimbs.

Denny dashed forward and picked up the stunstik dropped by the dasik Cousin Haw had hit. Then he ran back across the square and swung the stik toward the nearest of the remaining dasiks. The tall dasik saw him coming, and started to turn, but Denny's blow caught it solidly in the side. The stunstik emitted a buzzing noise and the dasik's yellow eyes went wide. It started to fall. Denny hit it again, just to be sure.

Omi had the next dasik pinned between two of his limbs. Denny leaped toward it, putting one foot on the downed Overcontroller's shell in passing, and managed to clip the dasik on one high shoulder. The blow wasn't enough to knock the dasik down, but its arm dangled limply and the stik fell from its hand. It looked at them for a moment, opened its long mouth, and made a very high, squeaky sound. Then it turned and dashed from the courtyard in the same direction the chug had taken, long feet slapping against stone.

Denny crouched down beside Omi. "Are you okay?"

The young cithian turned its eyepads toward him. "Denny. I didn't know. I didn't."

"It's all right," said Denny. "I know you didn't." He took Omi by the smooth section of a forelimb and tried to help him to his feet, but the cithian's right side was still numbed by the effect of the stunstik.

Voices sounded from the distance. Denny raised his head and saw that more ferries were arriving. The chug was coming back toward the square, and behind him was a crowd of figures that included cithians, dasiks, and even a pair of skynx. Closer to hand, Overcontroller Hiser was beginning to wave his limbs as he recovered from the shock Omi had delivered.

Denny spotted the Overcontroller's gun at the side of the yard. He ran to it. The weapon was large enough and heavy enough that it took both hands to raise it. He wasn't quite sure how it worked, but it seemed simple enough. He turned to face the approaching crowd and sighted down the thick barrel.

"Denny! No!" Omi tried to scramble to his feet, but fell again. "No."

"But..."

Omi waved a forelimb at the sign on the ground. "You came in peace. Go the same way."

Denny let the gun fall to the stones. "Come with us."

"No," said Omi.

From somewhere back down the path came a series of sharp cracking sounds. Denny heard something go singing through the air. More of the sounds followed. There was a loud ping as something bounced from the metal statue of the man.

With one last look at Omi, Denny turned and ran into the ship.

40

Just inside the door, everyone was huddled together in the center of a short hallway. There was another door not two steps ahead. It was firmly closed.

Talla looked at him. "We can't get this door to open, or the outside door to close."

"Yulia–" he started, then he noticed that Yulia was at the center of the group. She was lying on her back on the floor eyes closed.

Kettle looked up at him. "We can't get it out of her hand. It's like it's stuck."

Denny joined them. He could hear shouts from outside the ship. Another of those cracking noises sounded, and this time the ping of impact came from the ceiling just over his head. He lifted Yulia's hand. As Kettle had said, the silver maton seemed glued to her fingers. No matter how he touched it, Yulia's fingers wouldn't release their grip. The skin of her fingers looked bruised. Almost burnt. The edge of the little purple memory was jutting between her fingers. It was hot to the touch.

More shots sounded. They banged off the walls, the ceiling, the inner door. Cousin Haw gave a grunt and spun up against the wall. Denny saw a line of blood across the metal floor. Talla put herself in front of Sirah, wrapping herself around the younger girl, though Sirah struggled against it.

Denny stood and ran to the inner door. There was a panel to touch, but touching it did nothing. There were no other controls Denny could see. Only a small depression beside the panel. A small, square depression.

He ran back toward Yulia. Something punched him in the left arm, and lights seemed to flash inside his head. Denny tumbled to the floor beside Yulia. He reached for the maton, and turned it over until he found the point where the purple memory cube was visible between Yulia's fingers. Denny grabbed it, pulled it, and popped it free.

Denny got back to his feet. There was more blood on the floor now. It seemed like a lot. The snaps and bangs and pings came from everywhere. His shoe slipped in the blood as he was getting back to the door. The distance to the door seemed to have become almost infinitely long.

Not exactly leaving in peace, he thought. He raised the little cube. A shot banged off the wall beside him. The cube slotted into space. No figure appeared.

He turned toward the open door to the outside. The light of Tollsday seemed as red and bloody as the hallway. "Athena. Close the door. Athena!"

The door began to close.

41

PAIRDAY

On Pairday, Denny left Jukal Plex. They would have liked to wait longer. They would have liked to wait until Yulia was awake, until Denny and Haw were healed. Until they understood more about the massive ship. But they couldn't.

"If the other races defeated all the humans," said Talla. "You can bet they can handle a single old ship. We need to get away while we can."

Even so, it took time. Athena, who could appear to all of them now, was able to control the ship, but it took time to start the long cold engines. Time to wake systems that had been still for generations. Time to reconfigure the matons at the heart of the ship to accept the programming that Athena had for them.

There was an amazing amount of space inside the ship. It was far bigger inside than Denny's compartment building. There were rooms for sleeping and rooms for growing food and rooms for studying the stars and planets. It was a whole new plex.

Sirah sewed up Denny's arm and wrapped it in a tight bandage. "There," she said. "It looked bad, but you should be all right in a few days."

The room they were in was a room for healing. A "medical bay" according to the sign outside the door. It was still full of bandages and tools for healing. Medicines, too, though most of those they didn't yet understand. There were a number of beds in the room. On one of them was Yulia. She was still unconscious, and had been that way since they climbed into the ship. Athena said that she should recover, but Kettle still sat beside her bed, waiting. On another bed was Haw. Haw had been awake–awake enough to do a lot of shouting and swearing. Now he was asleep again. Among the few medicines Athena had explained to them was one that eased pain and brought on sleep. Considering how loud Haw had been, everyone was glad that Athena had passed on that knowledge.

The air in the middle of the room shimmered for a moment, and Athena appeared. She looked much as she had the last time Denny had seen her back in the house by the gate. A little bit of Yulia, a little bit of Sirah, a little bit of them all. But she looked different, too. Her face was no longer stuck in that half-smile. Her expressions, and the look in her eyes, seemed much more human.

"Talla thought you might want to come up to the viewing area," she said. "We're about to leave."

Sirah helped Denny down off the bed. "We'll be right there," she said. Athena disappeared.

Denny looked over at Kettle. "Are you coming?"

Kettle raised his head for a moment. "No. No, I think I'll stay here." He nodded toward Yulia. "Just in case."

Together, Sirah and Denny walked out into a long hallway, filled with clean light.

42

The ship, whose name was not actually Cataclysm, but Revelation, shook off the soil of the planet called Rask and rose up on a tower of lightning and thunder. It took only seconds before Jukal Plex was lost to sight, and seconds more before the whole planet was a green-gray dot, and seconds after that the red star and the blue star had merged together into a tiny purple-white point as the ship moved away, and away, and away.

43

WHETSDAY

On Whetsday, Denny danced between the stars.

About the Author

 Mark is the author of a bunch of novels, lots of short stories, and essays. His novel *Devil's Tower* was nominated for the World Fantasy Award, and his *News from the Edge* series was turned into a TV show called *The Chronicle*, which aired on the Syfy Network. Mark has held nearly every job known to man, including coal miner, USGS cartographer, newspaper photographer, and database architect. He has dug for dinosaurs in South Dakota. And he used to know the genus and species of every freshwater fish in the United States.

When he isn't writing or working or blogging, Mark enjoys paddling out on the lake in his kayak and watching the resident osprey hunt for his breakfast. The lake used to contain a lake monster, but Mark hasn't spotted him in a while.

Fun Fact

I wish I had good writing habits, but I don't. I don't write at a particular time. I don't write to a particular length. I get easily distracted. I find that I eat a ton of cereal when I'm writing. Always cereal. I don't care if it's Special K, Love Crunch Granola, or giant bags of Marshmallow Mateys (yes that's a real cereal). I down it at a rate of about a bowl a page. So my writing is extremely high in carbohydrates. Sometimes I stop eating cereal long enough to eat a plate of 1) hard bread, 2) dates, 3) dried mango, and 4) hard, sharp cheese. Those are the writing food groups: cereal, and dried fruit on a plate with cheese. Note that I can't promise that this will work for you in terms of making pages. However, it will solve any problem you're having with putting on weight.